MW00324570

"Courageous. Explosive. This life-after-death story of choice and how it determines the fate of an ordinary man is fictional, but it's impact is very real—soundly based on the ultimate standard of truth. A must-read." -Nanette O'Neal, author of *A Doorway Back to Forever: Believe.*

"Boldly written, intriguing and suspenseful. The kind of page-turning drama we've come to expect from Brenda Poulos. The tension builds with every chapter, sending the reader on a terrifying emotional rollercoaster. Brenda paints a vivid, shocking story—compelling, as it twists and turns—leaving one reading late into the night." – Kary Oberbrunner, author of *Your Secret Name* and *The Elixer Project.*

"*The Choice* will touch a cord with anyone whose loved one's heart has appeared to have hardened beyond all hope. Brenda Poulos weaves an imaginative tale with likable characters and a plot that many Christians will recognize as tragically realistic. You may have never read a story like *The Choice*, but my guess is that you or someone you know should read it before it is too late!" - Barbara Bras, author of *Wrapped in God's Grace, a Life Rediscovered* and *She Who Knows, a Tale of the Heart.*

"Brenda Poulos has created a cast of believable, engaging characters. I found myself bonding with them and longing to know more about their future, their struggles, and their relationship with each other, and with God." - Rebecca D. Bruner, author of *Welcome, Earthborn Brother* and *Sarah's Laughter.*

"The most important decision anyone will make in this life is whether to choose Jesus Christ to be their Savior or not. *The Choice* is the tale of one man's decision. As a Christian, it forced me to look inside myself to ask whether I've become complacent to the lost around me. Highly recommended reading." – Fran Veal, author of *Finding My Escape.*

THE CHOICE

Additional Books by Brenda C. Poulos
Runaways: The Long Journey Home

THE CHOICE

WILL'S LAST TESTAMENT

———◆———

Brenda C. Poulos

Copyright © 2016 Brenda C. Poulos
All rights reserved.
Printed in the United States of America
Published by Author Academy Elite
P.O. Box 43, Powell, OH 43035

www.AuthorAcademyElite.com

All rights reserved. No part of this publication may be reproduced, stored in a retrieval system, or transmitted in any form or by any means—for example, electronic, photocopy, recording—without the prior written permission of the publisher. The only exception is brief quotations in printed reviews.

ISBN: 1943526559
ISBN 13: 9781943526550
Library of Congress Control Number: 2016910375
Author Academy Elite, Powell, OH

To my sister, Peggy Zwerin.
You have been my constant friend and champion
from the days of Jacks and Jump ropes to the
Empty nest and Retirement Years.

And to my sister, Darlene Hall.
Your tender heart and gentle spirit exemplify
God's unconditional love.

ACKNOWLEDGEMENTS

———

My Beta readers helped give clarity and direction. I am thankful
for each of them: Lois Cuperus, Dolores Guadian,
Sue Moses, and Doris Sievers.

My critique group offered support and guidance, pushing me far
beyond my initial vision for this book. These amazing friends are:
Crystal Acosta, Karen Hsu, Nancy Johnson, and Dee Kincade.

"Enter through the narrow gate.
For the gate is wide and the road is broad that leads
to destruction, and many enter through it."

PROLOGUE

———◆———

THE WEATHER FORECAST HAD BEEN accurate. Already a storm was rolling in from the west. The sky was dark. Wind slapped wet leaves from the eucalyptus trees against the large windows overlooking the visitors' parking lot.

Will tossed his 15-slide puzzle onto the chair beside him, a scowl on his face. He had seen dozens of kids conquer it at school, but he'd never gotten more than ten numbers in consecutive order. What was he doing wrong? His mind was clearly not on the game—and not on celebrating his fourteenth birthday, today, either—it was on room 204, where his father lay fighting for his life.

He closed his eyes and leaned his head back against the waiting room wall. Why was the doctor taking so long? Running late, Will had missed the opportunity to visit with his father before school. Then, the ancient team van had broken down on the way back from the after-noon's track meet. It was now eight o'clock. Visiting hours would be over in thirty minutes. There would be hardly enough time to relay the happenings of the entire meet, as his father would expect.

Jim Hayes had been the picture of health last season but by mid-summer, dizzy-spells and a series of seizures had led to hospital tests and a diagnosis of a heart problem that just couldn't be fixed with surgery. Though now he was in the hospital hospice unit, Will refused to believe the end was inevitable.

There was still time for God to intervene...

Will bowed his head and sent up another prayer, pleading for his father's life. He begged God for more good times as a family and for restoration of the retirement years his father so looked forward to. Time for his father to spend traveling and ticking dreams, one-by-one, off his bucket list.

"God, please heal my dad. If you never answer another prayer the rest of my life, I will be okay with only this one. He's everything to me. I need him. So does Mom. I can't stand to see him suffer anymore. Please help the doctors figure this out. Please let Dad live."

Hearing footsteps on the tile floor, Will raised his head. When he saw his mother's pale face, he knew his father was gone.

No healing. No answered prayer. No thanks to God.

CHAPTER 1

———————

WILL STOPPED DEAD IN HIS tracks. It was love at first sight. His pulse raced as he watched a goddess close her eyes and tilt her face toward the early morning sun. He envied its warmth as it caressed her light brown hair. The hem of her flowered skirt fluttered in the morning breeze, dancing above her open-toed sandals.

A twig broke under Will's feet causing her to jump and turn in his direction. She looked up at him, a frightened rabbit in the midst of the university's cactus garden. He managed to hold her gaze for a brief moment before she gathered her books and half-ran toward the library steps.

Oh, no! I scared her. Will pushed back his ball cap and jogged in her direction, his chin-length blond hair falling into his eyes. Being on the track team gave him the advantage and he caught up with her after only three long strides. "Please." He touched her arm with his left hand, his right laden with textbooks. "I'm Will." His mouth went dry and he swallowed hard. "Can I talk with you a minute?"

The girl's eyes traveled up his lanky frame.

He sighed when, at long last, they met his for the second time. "Sorry I startled you. I'm not a predator or anything like that. I was just walking by and, well, I just——"

Her soft laughter coaxed a smile onto his face. "I'm Brigit. It's nice to meet you, Will."

"What? Really? You are—I mean—really glad to meet me?" Will blew out a long breath and shook his head. "Wow!" He needed to control himself or he'd come off looking like an idiot.

"Here. Care to sit?" Brigit led him to the steps. Sitting down herself, she patted a place on the hard concrete surface in the shade of a large Ocotillo. She shivered. "These steps are cold. Arizona's had an unusually long winter this year. It's normally warmer than this by the middle of March, isn't it?"

Will stumbled to her side and sat down at an arm's length. "I think so." He couldn't believe that this gorgeous girl would give him the time of day, but here he was perched beside her on the last day of classes before spring break.

"I recognize you. Advanced Biology? Mr. Jantzen?" Her lips framed perfect white teeth.

"Are you kidding? There's no way we went to the same high school. I would have definitely noticed *you*!" Will shook his head in disbelief, wondering where in the world she'd been hiding.

"It's the truth. Only you were officially in Jantzen's class. I was just his third period aide."

Will's face broke into a huge grin. "Unbelievable. Absolutely unbelievable."

Brigit glanced at her watch and gasped. "Oops. Gotta go. I work here in the library three hours a day and I'm already five minutes late." She started down the steps, and then turned around to give Will a quick wave.

"Wait." Will leapt down the two steps between them and caught her hand. "Can I have your number? I mean, would it be okay if I called you sometime—like maybe in three hours and five minutes?"

Brigit looked down at their hands, her small one caught in his slightly larger one. She took a deep breath, the warmth of her blush rising from her neck and onto her cheeks.

Will's heart skipped a beat as he released her fingers. "Sorry. I didn't mean to——"

Her laughter was contagious. "Do you have homework?"

Doesn't everyone? "Yeah, but——"

"Why don't you do your homework in the library, and then walk me back to my dorm after I'm done?" She raised her eyebrows and smiled, waiting for his answer.

She was certainly making this easy for him. Did his awkward demeanor suggest that he was already putty in her hands? "Sure. I can do that." He wouldn't tell her that he had a class in twenty minutes. Missing it would knock his grade down from a B to a C, since he'd already had two absences, but he'd gladly let that happen in the name of love.

———

Brigit stole a look in Will's direction every few minutes just to see if he was still at the study table. He could be a figment of her imagination, after all. She was sure he hadn't known about the secret crush she'd had on him in high school. In fact, she was certain he'd never even looked her way. Her thick glasses, braces, and bad case of acne had made her almost invisible to most of the guys at Tempe High.

Will looked up from his book, smiled, and wiggled his fingers in an almost imperceptible hello, then turned his attention back to his work. Her stomach flip-flopped. He was flirting with her!

He looked in her direction a few minutes later, scribbled something on his notepad and ripped it out. Then he walked up to the desk, placed the note on top of her book cart and sauntered back to his study table.

Her heart thumped so loud that she looked in Mrs. Percell's direction to see if she had heard it, too. Convinced that her supervisor's gaze remained glued to her task as she catalogued a new book shipment,

Brigit unfolded Will's note. His penmanship could use a little work, but that was a minor imperfection she'd overlook.

A few minutes later, she caught him staring in her direction. Her face turned hot as she nodded. Of course she would go for a burger at The Chuckbox. She wouldn't tell him that she'd had a burger every day for the past week. She'd eat frog's legs if it meant she'd have a chance to spend time with the ever-popular high school track star, Will Hayes.

———————

Three and one half hours later, Will led Brigit into The Chuckbox. The smell of burgers and ribs on the grill permeated the small space. It had rustic charm, with checkered tablecloths on picnic-style tables. A roll of paper towels on each one of them acted as self-serve napkins. They sat down at a booth near the back, away from the noise of the Juke Box.

Will's best friend since junior high school, Derf—Fred spelled backward—placed menus in front of them, then moved on to the next table to take their order.

As Brigit studied her menu, Will studied her. Her skin was flawless—almost translucent—and had no trace of makeup. She was a natural beauty. *What luck.* He wouldn't be kept waiting for hours in the living room while her little brother annoyed the life out of him, like always happened when he'd picked up his previous girlfriend.

All of a sudden, Will gulped, his eyes widening. "Oh, no. Is this Wednesday?" How could he have forgotten this? After all, Lanie had been talking about it for the past month.

"All day." Brigit frowned. "Why? Something wrong?"

"Um. Well, not really. I just have to make a phone call. It's no big deal." Will smiled a crooked smile, and then winced. He'd need to think up some good excuse.

Brigit folded her menu and sighed. "You have a date, don't you?"

"Not really. Well kind of, sort of—" Will attempted to buy some time as he tried to think what to do. Would he have to break the spell that surrounded them so soon? He'd much rather be here with Brigit than at Lanie Kingston's birthday luau.

Brigit slid out of her seat and stood facing Will. "I think you have a date. But, it's all right." She tucked a stray wisp of curly brown hair behind her ear. "I understand. We met and then...well, I should be studying right now, anyway. I've got a term paper I need to get started on." She headed toward the door.

Will hung his head. It wasn't like he and Lanie were going together. They'd known each other since grade school and were in each other's company a lot because their mothers were best friends. They often ended up doing things together if neither of them had a date. For the most part, he considered Lanie a good friend. There was nothing romantic there, but Brigit wouldn't know that unless he told her...

He threw a dollar bill on the table and hurried after Brigit. He looked in both directions when he got outside. She was nowhere in sight. *How could that girl have gotten that far in just the time it took me to—?* He felt a tap on his shoulder and turned around.

"You rushed right by. Didn't you see me?" Brigit's eyes sparkled as she laughed. She held out her hand as if she wanted to shake his.

"What's this?" Will was surprised by her sudden formality. This couldn't mean what he thought it did. He didn't want to let go of her hand, but she claimed it back with a small squeeze.

"This is good-bye and thank you for a lovely day. I hope to see you around again, sometime." Brigit hesitated, then reached up and gave him a brief kiss on the cheek. She flashed him one last smile before she turned away. "Oops, I forgot." She handed Will a folded paper towel and off she went.

Will's mouth hung open and the palm of his hand rested on his cheek as Brigit walked down the street, turned the corner, and vanished into the early afternoon sunshine. He hadn't even had a chance to explain about Lanie.

He unfolded the paper towel. Written in bright pink lipstick was Brigit's phone number. "Unbelievable. Absolutely unbelievable."

———◆———

Will felt around in the dark for the wall switch and flicked on the kitchen light. He turned the deadbolt to the locked position, placed the lei in the refrigerator, and filled a glass with water before walking up the stairs toward his room. After he closed the door, he clicked on the small desk lamp and placed the glass on a Denver Broncos coaster. He fell face down on his unmade bed.

What a day this had been. First, meeting Brigit and then the horrible fight with Lanie at her birthday party. It really hadn't been his fault. Lanie had picked the fight with him, fuming because he was late. He wasn't, though, because he had made it there right on the button. It was just that he had kind of promised to get there early to help with the helium balloons. So, he could see her point—sort of.

Would this be the end of his friendship with Lanie? Would Mom take her side? If Will was lucky, their mothers would remain friends, and he and Lanie would make up. He'd suggest they not see quite so much of each other in the future. After all, he wanted to devote most of his free time to getting to know Brigit. He looked again at her phone number and shoved the paper towel back into his pocket.

Will had made a huge mistake when he and Lanie kissed a few weeks ago. It was experimentation more than anything else for Will, but Lanie wanted more. She had assumed a few kisses meant they were going to be a couple, but when that didn't happen she'd been angry. She still was.

He reached over and set the clock radio for six o'clock. That should give him plenty of time to get to the bench outside the library and wait for Brigit to show up for work tomorrow morning. He'd apologize and grovel a little if that's what it took to get her to give him another chance. Would it be too tacky of him to take her the lei from Lanie's party? It still looked pretty good.

A soft knock at the door interrupted his thoughts. "Mom?"

His mother opened the door. She pushed her reading glasses onto her forehead and then rubbed the bridge of her nose. "I just finished the last chapter of my book so I thought I'd stick my head in and see how the party went." She smoothed back her shoulder-length gray hair and raised her eyebrows as she waited for his answer.

Will rolled over and then sat up on the side of the bed, stretching and giving a loud yawn. "Oh, it was okay."

His mother sat down in the molded plastic desk chair. "Did Lanie like her necklace?"

"Well, I...didn't give it to her." Will's shoulders drooped. "We had a fight about my getting there late—which I really didn't—and she basically kicked me out of the party before they even dug up the pig."

Mom gave Will a hug, then pulled back to look him in the eye. "I'm sorry that happened, but—"

"I know. I know. She's your friend's daughter, so somehow we've got to work it out for the good of everyone." Will looked away and rolled his eyes.

"Exactly. Besides it's—"

"The Christian thing to do." Why did she insist he use the C-word? Couldn't it be the *moral* thing to do? How about the *right* thing to do?

"Uh huh. Just because you say you aren't a believer, doesn't mean you can't follow Christian principles." She pursed her lips and stared at him a moment before continuing. "There's leftover pot roast in the fridge."

Will shook his head. "No. I'm not hungry. I stopped by The Chuckbox on the way home." He wished he'd stayed there in the first place, considering how he already felt about Brigit.

His mother stifled a yawn of her own as she headed for the door. "Well, at least you don't have to get up early tomorrow."

Will furrowed his forehead and threw his mother a quizzical look.

"Spring break, you know."

Will's hand went to his pocket. Brigit must not be working tomorrow. That's why she gave me her number! He glanced at the clock. Ten-thirty. Would she still be awake?

———•———

CHAPTER 2

BRIGIT FIDGETED AS SHE SAT at the same table she and Will had shared the day before. Imagine. She had a certifiable lunch date with someone she'd had a massive crush on in high school. This just couldn't be happening! But it was...

Her weekends back then had been pretty lonely. Her two best friends, Sue and Mary Ellen, were cheerleaders and had games to attend, as well as lots of dates with school jocks. Brigit could have been more social, but she chose to stay at home, playing monopoly with her parents or reading Mary Higgins Clark mysteries.

That all changed on May 1, 1975. It was near the end of her junior year of high school when she saw Will Hayes walk down the hallway. She was smitten. She spent the following year at cross country track meets, basketball games, and even school dances—any place she thought he might be. Odds were he'd have to look in her direction at some point in the 200 days until graduation. When he did, she'd be ready to flash him a perfect smile—the one she practiced every night in her bedroom mirror.

She had all but given up the hope of ever having even the briefest conversation with him, so it was remarkable that they'd meet face-to-face five years later in front of the university library only months before college graduation. She looked at her watch. Where was he? It was already a quarter past twelve.

Tall, dark-haired Derf approached her table. "Will just called and said to tell you he got a flat tire a couple of blocks from here. He's going to walk on over. Should be here in a few minutes."

"Thanks, Derf."

Derf cocked his head. "You know my name?"

"Sure. We went to school together. Brigit Dawson? Freshman English? Mrs. Dean gave you that name because we had *two* Fred's in our class."

Derf's face turned crimson. "That's right. It stuck, too. Even my parents still call me Derf." He stroked his chin. "Dawson. Dawson. Rick's sister?"

"The one and only." She couldn't restrain her laughter. Had she been invisible to *everyone?*

"Well, I'll be…you don't look like her. She—" Derf's smiled faded, his demeanor turning serious. "Hey, sorry about Rick. He was—"

"Thanks, but I'd rather not talk about it." Ever. She couldn't think about it or she'd… She blinked back an unexpected tear.

Will stuck his head around the corner and swung into the seat opposite Brigit. Sweat had formed a band around his Broncos cap. His face was smudged with dirt and grease. "I'm sorry I look—and smell—so bad. I didn't want to take time to go home to shower and risk your leaving, so I just came as I was." He tore off a piece of paper toweling and attempted to wipe the grime from his face and arms.

"That's okay. I've just been passing the time with Derf, here, talking about old times." Brigit smiled at Derf as he pointed his right index finger at her and winked.

Will cleared his throat. "Looks like you've got a line of people waiting at the register, Derf. Now get outta here. You've already got a girlfriend."

Derf raised his shoulders in resignation and headed back to work.

Brigit couldn't help laughing. Those two must have been friends for a long time. They were fun to watch. They reminded her of Andy and Barney on The Andy Griffith show. She cleared her throat and tried to get the image of Will as the sheriff and Derf as his sidekick out of her head. "So, do you think you ran over a nail?"

"I'm pretty sure someone slit the tire."

"Why would they do that? I mean, that's pretty malicious, isn't it?" Brigit bit the inside of her cheek.

"Yeah—and expensive. I hope I stopped soon enough that it didn't ruin the rim." Will's face twitched as he shook his head.

Brigit's hand tingled when she placed it on his. "That's a pretty serious prank."

"It was no prank. I have a good idea who did it, but I'll probably never be able to prove it." Will drummed his fingers on the table.

"So, a man with enemies, huh?" Brigit pushed her drink toward Will. "You must be thirsty. Have mine. I'll order another." Will grinned. "Thanks! If you're sure..." He downed it all at once. "I think it was Lanie—or one of her friends—trying to get back at me. She says she's a Christian, but she sure doesn't act like one."

"How is a Christian supposed to act?" Brigit asked, her face solemn.

"Oh, no. I should have seen it coming. You're one of *them*!" Will pushed the cup aside and went for his wallet. "Of all the luck."

Brigit reached over and grabbed him by the arm. "Wait. Why would you think that?"

Will gave her a quizzical look. "You mean you're *not* a Christian?"

"Well, not in the sense that *you* mean. I believe that God *exists*. That maybe he even did create this world. But do I go to church? No. Do I pray? No. Do I think that God knows me or cares about *me*? Not really. I think it's like the song says 'He's watching us from a *distance*.' He doesn't really love us. If he did, he'd protect us. He wouldn't let people get hurt or die..."

Will ripped off some paper toweling and offered it to her. "Here."

Brigit blotted away escaping tears. She shouldn't get so emotional. He'd think she was a nut case. No reason to go into all of it just now— or ever for that matter.

"Sorry." He ran his index finger along the top of her hand. "I agree. If God doesn't care about us, then why should we care about him? As far as I'm concerned we've covered the 'God topic' as thoroughly as we need to. Don't get me wrong. I want to be a good person and live a life that will make a difference in our world. I just don't need *his* help to do it."

Brigit smiled and shook her head in agreement. "Hey. I'm starving. Let's see if we can get Derf to take our orders." She made a circle with her thumb and index finger and placed it in her mouth, producing a high-pitched whistle that stopped all conversation in the small restaurant. "Derf!"

———◆———

Four hours, three sodas, and one large burger later, Will had learned all the important stuff his mother would be sure to ask about this new girl. Brigit's parents had relocated back east just a few months earlier to be near their daughter-in-law, Angie, and her newborn twins. They'd given Brigit the option of moving into a dorm and staying at Arizona State, or going with them and attending a smaller eastern college and living at home.

She'd chosen to remain at ASU. Without money to do much else, she was staying in Tempe for spring break. She'd probably visit her parents over the summer vacation, see their home, and meet her nephews. They'd be almost a year old by then.

At the end of May, Will and Brigit would both turn twenty-two. They shared the same astrological sign—Gemini. Neither one had committed to a political party. At this point it wasn't of importance to either of them. They both liked living in the southwest where they could swim, hike, and roller skate—all activities that lent themselves to warmer climates.

Will and Brigit strolled down the street, walking in the direction of the cactus garden where they had met the day before. "I like this area. In the three and a half years I've been at this school, this is only the second time I've been over here."

"It's funny, isn't it, that we don't always see what's right under our very noses." Brigit pulled Will to sit on the bench, facing a small pond of water.

Will studied the right side of Brigit's face. "Yes, funny how that happened."

Brigit's cheeks flushed. She cleared her throat. "I really love this spot, too. When I'm feeling down, I come here to help me think. I'm usually in a better frame of mind by the time I walk back to the dorm." Her voice trailed off as she turned her attention to feeding some birds leftover pieces of her hamburger bun.

Will stood and reached for her hand. "Feel like walking some more? I need to put the spare tire on and get my car out of the church parking lot."

"Really? A *church* parking lot?" Brigit's mouth dropped open and she blinked her eyes several times.

"Can you believe it? Hope it's not prayer meeting night. Someone might get all bent out of shape if I'm in their parking spot." With a playful wink, he tugged on her hand and started jogging down the sidewalk, past the huge fountain and the library, in the direction of his car parked on Ash Avenue.

"Hey, I'm not in cross country, you know. Slow down or I'll never make it!" Brigit pulled Will to a stop in front of the Language and Literature building. "I need to catch my breath. I didn't know I was so out of shape." Brigit bent over, hands on her knees, sucking in the late afternoon air.

"All right, wimp, but you're going to have to get with the program if you're planning on hanging out with me over spring break." He smiled and tapped the end of her nose with his forefinger. "Tomorrow morning. Bright and early. You and me. A surprise outing. What do you say?" They'd take a motorboat ride around Saguaro Lake. Maybe he could get his mom to help him put together a little picnic lunch for afterward. Then they could find a nice relaxing spot to spend the afternoon...

"How do you know I'm not busy?" Brigit teased.

Will hesitated. "Well, are you?"

"You never know. I might have planned a full day at the library, working on my Lit 4 term paper." A sly smile played on her lips.

"How could writing a term paper possibly compare with spending time with me? Fresh air...sunshine?" Will dropped down on one knee and put his hands together, begging.

"You look so pitiful down there. I guess if it doesn't have anything to do with running, I'll have to take you up on your offer. Besides, I've always been a sucker for surprises."

"Then it's a date. Nine o'clock?" He'd have to remember to reschedule the game of racquetball with Derf. He was probably getting tired of Will beating him, anyway.

"I'll be ready, but you'd better get up from there. We've got a crowd gathering and I'm sure they're misinterpreting what you're doing." Her outstretched arm motioned toward a small group of students with huge smiles plastered on their faces.

Will looked around in all directions. It might be crazy, but he could fast forward in his mind and see himself on bended knee in the future—only then he *would* be posing a completely different question —the one their audience thought he was asking Brigit right now.

CHAPTER 3

———◆———

CLOSING HIS EYES FOR A moment, Will took in a deep breath before he picked up the razor and faced the mirror. The morning breeze, wafting through the open bathroom window, held the promise of a memorable spring day. He hadn't been this excited about anyone in a long time. Forty-eight hours ago, he'd had no plans for spring break, much less for the rest of his life. But that had all changed.

He *never* went to the library. He *never* cut across the middle of campus. But on Wednesday, he'd been running late and for some reason he'd taken the shortcut. He would have made up for lost time, too, if it hadn't been for that engaging smile…

He drew the razor across his face in a crisscross pattern, starting with his right cheek, across his chin to his left cheek, and the full length of his upper lip, ending back where he had started—just like he'd seen his father do so many times. He ran the faucet and held a washcloth under it until it got hot. He squeezed it out, and with one quick motion, wiped the shaving cream from his face. *Whew! That would wake anybody up.*

He studied himself in the mirror. Was he as good-looking as his dad had been? Mom thought so. But moms always say that to their sons, looking at them through the eyes of love and all that. He and his dad had the same square chin and slender nose, but James Hayes had had dark brown hair and eyes, whereas Will's eyes were crystal blue and his hair a sun-streaked blond.

He combed his wet hair back with his fingertips. Funny. His dad used to do that, too. Why'd he have to die so young? This was the time Will needed a dad most. Just as he was about to graduate, get a job, and perhaps marry. There was so much he could have shared with him. Not that he needed the whole birds and the bees talk. No, it was about stuff like sharing halftime chatter or fishing off the pier until sundown and never saying a word. Moms just didn't understand. Apparently God didn't either.

He felt his face twitch and looked down at his balled up fists—two telltale signs that he was still unable to think about his father without getting upset. Maybe he was making too much out of it, but meeting Brigit had made him all sappy and sentimental for some reason. Like he was about to turn a corner. He was excited to see what was around it, but hesitant at the same time.

What if he needed someone to lean on?

———◆———

At exactly nine o'clock, Brigit stood by the window of the dorm's living room, waiting for Will to pull up to the curb in his bright red Mustang. He'd bought a new tire on the way home yesterday. What would make Lanie do such a vindictive thing? She wanted to ask him about her. Was she an old girlfriend—or perhaps a current one?

Mary Ellen had once said Will was drop dead gorgeous—and she was right. Brigit knew it was his *appearance* that attracted her to him in the first place. But the hallway gossip mill seemed to agree that he wasn't popular just because he was cute or a track star. He was a nice guy. Polite. Respectful. Funny.

Part of her job as Mr. Jantzen's aide had been to straighten up his room between classes. She had always started with the chairs in row four—Will's row—just so she could catch the lingering scent of his cologne. She'd close her eyes for a moment and imagine what it would be like to sit beside him in his car and drive off into the sunset.

Now, as she stared out the window for the hundredth time, she saw the guy that had dominated her thoughts for so long pull up to the curb. Her instincts told her that he would turn out to be more than just a handsome face. She hoped his presence in her life would divert her thoughts from Rick and help her put this past year behind her. Maybe with Will as a distraction, she would be able to distance herself from the memory of what had happened to the brother she had loved so much. She grabbed her windbreaker, imaging the whole world watching as she ran down the sidewalk toward the Mustang.

———◆———

Will looked at Brigit's tennis shoes as she paced back and forth on the pier at Saguaro Lake while they waited for their rental motorboat to be pulled around. The spotless toes and clean soles told him that she either spent all her time studying or wasn't as much of an outdoors person as she had led him to believe. So much for future dates hiking and roller-skating.

She hadn't been talkative, or even looked at him, since they'd retrieved their belongings from the car. *And what's with this constant pacing?* Will grabbed her arm, turning her toward him. "Is everything okay?"

"Why wouldn't it be?" She kept her eyes fixed on the wooden planks beneath her as they swayed in the wakes of the boats coming in and out of the marina.

"Hey, Brigit, look at me." When she raised her chin, he used his thumbs to brush off the tears streaming down both cheeks. What could have caused this? Was it something he'd said? "Hey, what's the matter? I'm sorry if I—"

She covered her mouth with her hand and began to shake as she cried. "It's not...your...f-f-fault. You couldn't...possibly...know..." She took a step backward and looked up at him.

He put his hands on her shoulders and drew her to him, his chin resting on the top of her head. "Want to talk about it? It might help."

She nodded and wiped her eyes on the collar of her polo shirt. At the sound of the motorboat approaching, she pulled back. "Okay. Later. Here's the boat."

He hesitated to let her go. He was intoxicated by her perfume—Gardenia just like his mother wore—and her softness. He closed his eyes and sighed. She was so sweet, so vulnerable, and so sad. *What—or who—was responsible for that?* His hands balled into familiar fists at his sides.

He put the folding chairs, the cooler, and his grandmother's checkered tablecloth into the boat and then offered his hand to Brigit. She trembled as she stepped into it. Maybe she was afraid of water. He had no idea what else could it be. He looked back at her. "Are you uncomfortable on the water? I mean, you can swim, can't you?"

"I know how to swim. It's just that—" She shook her head. Newly-formed rivulets of tears followed familiar pathways down her cheeks.

Will looked past her in the direction of the marina employee, a rotund teenager with freckles and a nametag with *Big Jim* written on it. "You know what? I think we're just going to skip the boat ride." He reached for the cooler. "It's already eleven. We'll eat an early lunch at a picnic area and maybe take a walk afterward."

Jim shrugged. "Hey, no problem. We've got far fewer boats than people who want to rent them. It'll be gone in ten minutes. Guaranteed."

Will helped Brigit out of the boat and handed her the tablecloth. He put the chairs under his arms, picked up the cooler and led the way back to the car.

"You really don't have to do this." Brigit's face half-frowned, half-smiled as she brushed away lingering tears with her fingertips.

"We're here to have a good time and get to know each other. We can't do that if something's bothering you." He knew she was concerned about ruining the day for him, but he was worried about *her*.

———◆———

Will drove in silence, looking for the turn-off leading to a quiet spot he'd been to the summer before. When he saw the open gate and the winding road leading down toward the Verde River, he knew he'd found it. He drove on another couple hundred feet, dust from the dry road swirling around the car until he parked it at a small roadside area under a stand of cottonwood trees. Tall purple mountains encircled the entire area. It was picture perfect—peaceful, yet majestic at the same time.

He turned to Brigit, noticing that a frown still dominated her features. "You haven't said a word since we left the marina. Please don't think I'm mad at you. Just a little perplexed." He winked. "Come on. I'm starving!"

He hopped out, opened the trunk and lifted out the cooler. Mom had come through again. They had worked side by side for several hours earlier that morning, making all of Will's favorite foods. The fact that she had put in all that work for him and a girl he had only recently met, made him feel bad that he hadn't been completely honest in answering all her questions.

He'd hedged most of them except for the inevitable one about Brigit possibly being a Christian. His forceful "no" had put an end to their conversation. His mother had finished packing the basket, handed it to Will, and then turned her attention toward the sink of dirty dishes.

Brigit peered into the trunk. "Wow! You must've been up at the crack of dawn to put all this together. And you even brought a portable radio?" Her playful smile was back on her face where it belonged.

Heat rushed up Will's neck. Maybe he'd gone a little overboard. "Well, I'd like to take credit for all of this, but my mom actually fried the chicken and made the potato salad. She did let me bake the choco-late chip cookies, though—under her supervision, of course."

"Please tell her thank you for me." Brigit grabbed the quilt and walked toward the picnic table. "Did you happen to bring bug spray? The table is crawling with ants."

"No, but I always have a backup plan." He took her arm and spun her around.

"And what's that?"

Her slow smile melted away any defenses he still had intact. "We'll spread out Grandma's tablecloth and eat on the hood of the car." His heart double beat. He cleared his throat and offered her his hand. "Seating is now available for Hayes, party of two."

As Brigit settled on the hood next to him, Will leaned back against the windshield, looking toward the southern face of the mountain and beyond it to Four Peaks. "Some people like a landscape of trees and green grass, but me—I love our Arizona desert."

"It really is beautiful up here. Thanks for going to all this trouble and for changing your original plan after I—"

He put a finger to her lips and then began to unload the cooler. "My stomach is growling. Hand me your plate, little lady. We'll have plenty of time to talk about that after lunch."

———

After eating, Brigit followed Will on a barefoot walk down by the river. She had heard that last summer the county had trucked in tons of sand to line the riverbank, but nearly all of it had already washed away. Just enough remained to keep their feet from getting scraped by the rocky ground underneath.

The flowers that had budded out atop the giant saguaros looked like the Easter bonnets her young cousins wore in the picture Mom had sent. They looked happy and cheerful. Why shouldn't they be? Their family was still intact.

The early afternoon sun reflected off the water, making it almost impossible to see Will's face. Maybe it would make talking about Rick easier. "I think I owe you an explanation for my behavior back at the boat dock." She slipped her hand into his.

"You don't *owe* me one, but I am concerned, and I want to help you—if you'll let me." He let go of her hand and put his arm around her shoulders. They walked on, leaving their footprints behind on the damp earth.

"Last spring, my brother, Rick, and his wife, Angie, planned a water skiing trip on Lake Pleasant. They let me tag along. There were six of us—four guys, Angie, and me."

Brigit paused, took a deep breath, and then continued. "We rented a boat, bought a bunch of snacks at the marina, and then took off." She dabbed at her eyes with a tissue. Her stomach was in knots and her voice began to waiver. "This is so hard to talk about."

"Take it slow. There's no hurry." His crystal blue eyes encouraged her to continue.

They walked on for a few minutes in silence before she picked up the story again. "I'd never been skiing before, so I watched everyone else and I went last." A flood of haunting memories rushed into her consciousness: the wind being knocked from her as she hit the water, kelp twisting around her legs, the motor churning up the water as the boat turned and headed back in her direction. Then something hit her head so hard that blackness blotted out all memory of what happened next. Maybe she wasn't ready to talk about this after all. She pulled away from Will, stumbling up a rocky path.

When he caught up with her, he scooped her up in his arms. He carried her to higher ground and set her on a flat gray boulder at the entrance of a small cave. Its walls were covered in graffiti: *Bobby and Lisa were here. If this was your first time leave the date. Think before you...*

Brigit laid her head on his shoulder, her hand trailing back and forth on the rock's smooth surface. "I didn't even get to stand up on my skis before I wiped out. When I regained consciousness, they told me a ski had smacked me in the head and Rick jumped in to get me. His stomach cramped while he was still in the water."

Will shook his head. "I'm so sorry this happened, but you do understand that no one was to blame, don't you? It was just a horrible accident."

Brigit's face was bathed in tears. "But, he drowned saving *me*."

———◆———

Brigit took a long, hot shower in the deserted dorm bathroom. She let the water run as long as she wanted, knowing she didn't have to hurry so someone else could have a turn. Most of the girls had gone home to spend time with their families over the break. Being able to shower in privacy—and at her leisure—was a luxury.

She had worried needlessly. Will ended up being nothing but supportive as he listened to her account of the accident. He had been patient with her as she paused the story several times to regain control of herself and continue on. How had he known she harbored guilty feelings...and how important it was for her to get them out in the open?

Dealing with those emotions would still be hard, but she had promised him she would keep taking baby steps toward that end. He said he could already see a big difference in her—and she could *feel* what he could *see*. An immense weight had been taken off her shoulders, making it possible for her to look forward to the future and her budding relationship with Will.

The week ahead would be exciting. After returning from the river, they had stopped at The Chuckbox for a root beer float and mapped out the rest of spring break. They tried to be creative in planning things that didn't cost too much money, such as helping distribute water bottles at the local Special Olympics, taking a five-mile bike ride, joining some of his friends for a barbecue, as well as going to Will's house for dinner with his mother at the end of the week.

She admitted to herself that she was a little nervous about meeting Gretchen Hayes. Will had already filled her in on his doting mother, a single parent for the last eight years. He had told Brigit that she was a devoted—and often outspoken—Christian, often making it difficult for others who did not share her faith to get close to her. It was important to Brigit that Mrs. Hayes like her, so she hoped she didn't ask too many personal questions—especially those about religion and her family.

More relaxed than she had been in months, her thoughts returned to Will. Would it be wrong for her to find her own happiness so soon after Rick's death? Might others think she'd never really cared for him as deeply as she had?

She stepped out of the shower, grabbed her towel, and began to dry her hair. It was naturally curly, so she'd just let it dry the rest of the way on its own. She stared into the ceiling-to-floor mirror. Would her friends see anything different about her? Would they be able to guess that something monumental had happened? She watched as a flush ran the full length of her body.

It had been completely spontaneous.

Would she regret it, tomorrow?

Had it been too soon?

CHAPTER 4

———◆———

TWISTING HER FINGERS BACK AND forth, Brigit waited for the doctor in the small exam room at the university clinic. She pressed the Band Aid back into place in the crook of her arm and then clutched the paper gown to her chest. She looked down at her legs covered in goose bumps. *Why are medical offices always so cold?*

The room looked more like a storeroom than what it really was. Boxes of cotton squares, disposable gloves, and syringes were stacked against the wall several rows high. She'd never been fond of dentists or doctors, but she was far more anxious about this visit than any she could ever remember. She took a long breath to slow her rapid heartbeat.

She turned her head in the direction of the door when it opened. The doctor came in, shutting it behind him. He perched on a black leather stool, pushed his horn-rimmed glasses onto his forehead and looked her straight in the eyes. "It's as you suspected. You're two months along, according to my calculations."

A gasp escaped her lips. "It was a mistake. We didn't mean to…at the time, I never thought that—"

The doctor shook his head. "I know, my dear. I've heard it all before."

He doesn't know me. I'm not like that. She raised her voice to protest. "But, you don't understand. I would never have even—"

"Look, here are the business cards of two OB-GYNs that are good and within walking distance of the university. Make an appointment with one of them. They'll get you on some prenatal vitamins and let you know what to expect at each stage in your pregnancy. They'll give you information on adoption, if you decide to go that route. And, there's also a Planned Parenthood office a few blocks from here, if you want to—"

Brigit's hands shook as she took the cards. "I guess I thought *you* could help me."

"I could have, if you'd come here for contraceptive advice. But it's a little too late for that *now*. Don't you think?"

———

Finals week. Brigit hadn't seen Will for five days. She had decided to wait to talk to him. She'd have never been able to forgive herself if her news had caused him to flunk his final exams and kept him from graduating. As it was, she had a hard time studying, herself. Between the constant wandering of her mind back to the afternoon at the lake, intermittent bouts of morning sickness, and daydreaming about the baby, she got little accomplished.

She told Sue and Mary Ellen about the baby when they met for a late lunch after their practical exams. They said they had already guessed that she was pregnant from observing the way she had left class several times in the middle of lectures and the fact that she hadn't wanted to go for their usual morning run for the past several weeks.

"Of the three of us, you've always been the responsible one. What happened?"

Sue's innocent brown eyes asked the same question Brigit had asked herself so many times since her doctor's visit. "I—we—it's hard to explain. I told him about my brother's death. He was comforting me one minute and the next...it *just happened*."

Mary Ellen, the most progressive-thinker of the trio—and the most straightforward in voicing her opinions—fished in her wallet for a moment before thrusting a crumpled business card into Brigit's hand. "Take it from one who knows, you two haven't been dating long enough to turn this situation into a committed relationship. You don't even have to tell Will. This is the kind situation that pushes guys into a corner. It will doom your chances with him. Do the responsible thing."

Brigit looked down at the card. It had been folded and unfolded several times. Turning it over, she read the note scribbled on the back in purple ink: *1:00 p.m. Saturday the 9th*. She raised her eyes to meet her friend's. Her breath caught in her throat, recalling her own feelings as she'd driven Mary Ellen home from the clinic last spring...the vacant look in her friend's eyes...the paleness of her skin as she curled up in the back seat, tears trickling down her cheeks.

Lunch had ended with hugs and tears. Their friendships were changing and they knew it. Mary Ellen would spend the next two years as a nurse in the army and Sue would be moving to New York to pursue acting. Unlike Mary Ellen and Brigit, getting her nursing degree was just a back-up plan mandated by Sue's parents before they would agree to let her follow her dream.

And then there was Brigit's baby...

Confused and uncertain about the future, Brigit knew one thing. Will deserved to know. It was his baby, too. It was only right that he help make this decision. Maybe Mary Ellen's decision had been right for her, but somewhere deep inside Brigit there was a tiny flicker of hope...

Brigit remembered several soap operas she had seen, depicting clever ways the expectant mother had broken the news to the baby's father. She finally chose one, visited a nearby bookstore, and headed toward the cactus garden.

Will was waiting for her with a huge grin on his face. He kissed her on the cheek and pulled her down to sit beside him on "their" bench. "I sure missed you. Finals go okay?" He wrapped his arm around her shoulders.

"Yes. Fine. And yours?" She clutched the folded paper sack to her chest.

"Studying pays off. Exams were a cinch." His dimples punctuated his quick smile.

"That's good. I wished I'd studied more, but I—" She shook her head. *My grades won't be good enough for graduate school, now. And anyway, who am I kidding? With a baby to take care of, I won't be able to continue going to school.*

"If you haven't been studying, what have you been doing all week? I mean that was the point of not seeing each other, right? So we could study?"

"Yes..." She lowered her head, her eyes coming to rest on the brown bag in her hands.

He frowned, and then narrowed his eyes. "You've been all jittery since you got here. I can't imagine what it is, unless...Wait—are you breaking up with me? Is that it?" He stood up, walked a few feet away, and then turned back to look at her.

She pushed her bangs away from her face and looked up at the ancient Saguaro. "No, of course not. I just couldn't concentrate. I've had so much on my mind."

When he returned to sit beside her on the bench, he took her hands in his. "Like?"

"Well...I...kind of...oh, here!" She thrust the bag toward him. Her legs bounced up and down as she waited for him to open it.

He squinted his eyes at her, frowning like someone smelling rotten eggs. "What's this?" He unfolded the sack and let the book drop onto his lap. He stared at it for a few moments before looking up at her with wide eyes. "*What to Name the Baby?*"

She gulped. "We have about seven months to decide." *Why is he just sitting there?* She stood and clutched her stomach. *The girls were right. It's too soon for him.* "Say something. I've waited two weeks to tell you. I can't wait any longer."

Will's face paled. "The one and only time we——" His shoulders slumped, the book sliding to the ground.

"Yeah," she whispered. "Saguaro Lake."

His posture stiffened, his eyes dazed. "You're p-p-pregnant?"

She nodded, tears starting to form in the corners of her eyes.

"Are you sure? I mean, have you been to a doctor?" He grabbed her hands, guiding her to sit back down beside him.

She let her eyes meet his. "Yes. Two weeks ago, like I said."

He frowned and cocked his head to the side. "And you kept it to yourself all this time?"

She took in a deep breath. "I wanted you to take your finals without worrying about me or the baby or what to do."

"What do you mean by 'what to do'?"

She closed her eyes and let out a long sigh before facing him again. When she'd talked to her mother, she'd suggested Will and Brigit get married right away. Brigit had surprised even herself when she told her mother that a baby wasn't the reason to rush into marriage. "Nothing in particular. Just that...oh, I don't know...I guess that the future just looks different, now."

"You *do* want to have this baby, don't you?" His voice, soft and tender, lifted her hopes.

"I...I——"

"My baby…our baby…I'm asking you if you want to have it…keep it…raise it?" Will was crying now himself and making no effort to wipe the tears away.

"Now that I'm used to the idea and have thought about how having a baby will impact my life…and in spite of how hard it might be, financially…yes…I want to have your baby."

He grabbed her and held her tight. "Me, too." His whole body shook.

Did I hear him right? He wants the baby? When she felt him relax, she wiggled loose from his embrace and looked him in the eyes. "Really?"

"You seem surprised. Maybe I'm a little surprised, myself, but, yes, I want you to have our baby. It's kind of soon in our relationship, but I think we can handle it. I can't imagine my life without you and little whoever this is that's growing in there." He put a cautious hand on her belly and smiled.

She let out an enormous sigh. "Oh, Will, you have no idea what a relief this is for me." *As long as I know he wants the baby too, I can face anything that comes along.*

"I'm sorry you felt you had to keep this to yourself, but from this point on, I'm here for you and the baby. One hundred percent." His kiss was long and tender.

"Thank you for understanding. Neither one of us planned it. Neither one of us took…precautions. Like I told the doctor, it just happened and I—"

He clasped his hands to his chest. "I bet he got a good laugh when you said that!"

She felt her face flush. "What do you mean?"

"He probably thought you were a little old not to know how this happened…" He winked and gave her a playful nudge.

"You're laughing at me!" She pushed her bottom lip into a pout.

"No, no. I'm sorry. It's just the way you said it, that's all." He swung his arm around her shoulders and pulled her close. "Let's celebrate with a burger. My treat."

She nodded, fresh tears rolling down her cheeks.

His eyes widened. "What did I say?"

"Nothing." She looked up at him, brushing the tears away. "It's just that I had imagined all the things you *could* have said, but didn't. Instead, you said the one thing I wanted to hear most of all—that you want this baby, too."

———◆———

Will dried the dishes one at a time as his mother pulled them out of the rinse water and handed them to him. The past week had been torture. Each day Brigit asked if he had told his mother about the baby and each time he had come up with some excuse why he had not. *Tonight's the night, no matter what.*

His mother had continued their conversation from dinner about Lisa Kingston, hoping that her daughter, Lanie, and Will would be on friendly enough terms to join their mothers on their traditional June camping trip. He placed the last plate in the cupboard. *I can't listen to this for another minute. I promised Brigit. I need to quit stalling.*

"Will, have you heard a word I've said?" She let the water drain from the sink and rolled the sleeves of her silk blouse down, buttoning them at her wrists. "Lisa grilled Lanie about your tire. Seems an over-zealous boy hoping to make a big impression on her was responsible. Lisa's going to speak with his parents about him paying for it. In spite of everything, we all still want to go on the camping trip."

"But, Mom, *I* don't."

She frowned. "Surely you can patch things up with Lanie, can't you? You know how much our friendship means to me."

"Yes, Mom. I do. My not wanting to go has *nothing* to do with our fight. It has *everything* to do with Brigit." He ran his fingers through his hair, closed his eyes and took a calming breath.

"Let's sit and talk about this." His mother pulled out a yellow vinyl chair with chrome legs and motioned for him to sit next to her at the Formica-topped table. "Do you mean Brigit would be jealous?" She put one elbow on the table, resting her chin in her hand.

He hesitated. "She might. After all, the trip is two full weeks." He adjusted himself in his chair, folding and unfolding his hands on the tabletop.

"It's obvious there's something else on your mind...something rather serious from the look in your eyes and your constant fidgeting." Her smile encouraged him to speak.

He cleared his throat and looked straight at her. *I guess I might as well blurt it out.* "Yes, but I want you to remain calm until I finish talking and then you can—"

Her hand flew to her chest. "She's pregnant! Oh, my Lord, that's what this is about, isn't it? Oh, goodness. Tell me it's not true!"

Will put his elbows onto the table and lowered his head into his cupped hands. *I knew she'd take it hard. And, now for the lecture.* "Mom—"

"I can't believe it. I was sure you knew about these things...how to prevent..." She shook her head. "No. I'm sorry. I should have talked to you. I just kept putting it off and now, well... what a mess." She smoothed and re-smoothed her pleated skirt.

He raised his head to look in his mother's misty eyes. "I can hardly believe it myself, but...well...it's not like we planned it or anything... it just kinda happened..."

His mother jaw fell open. "It just *kind of happened?*"

His lips curled upward. He shook his head and laughed. *I can't believe I said the very words that—"*

"I don't think this is so funny, Will!" She raised her eyebrows and tilted her head.

"No, no. You don't understand. It's just that when Brigit told me about her conversation with the doctor, I…oh, never mind." He raked his fingers through his hair.

She crossed her arms, her mouth a firm line. "This is a matter you should take seriously, William Hayes. The course of your future—all of our futures—is about to change based on what you do about this problem."

"Problem?"

"Well, that word was not well chosen." She leaned forward, placing a hand on his arm. "What I mean is simply that, well, you have choices to make."

"You're not going to say I should force her to get an abortion, are you?" *That's probably what she wants. Keep it nice and quiet so none of her friends ever find out.*

"Now, Will, you know I would never suggest ending a life—not ever!"

"I'm glad to hear that because Brigit and I have decided to put—"

"It up for adoption." His mother sighed and relaxed her shoulders.

He grabbed her hand. "No, why would you think that?"

Her chin quivered. "I just finished the sentence with what I thought to be a logical ending."

"Well, it's not a logical ending to me. What I was going to say is that we are going to put our plans for grad school on hold, get jobs, move into an apartment together and raise our baby." He pressed his lips together, his jaw set.

"But, think of the child, Son." She placed her hands on his. "You're not ready to provide for a family. If you let the baby be adopted, it can live with a loving family and you can keep on track with your plans for graduate school and a career. Brigit's future is important, too. She'd be able to pursue her training to be a physician's assistant and—"

He banged a fist on the table. "Hold on. Hold on. First of all, this is *our* baby we're talking about and *we* are the loving family he'll live with."

She jerked back. "Will—"

He put his palms on the table, leaned forward, and shoved his face toward hers. "And, secondly, you mentioned *our* plans, but isn't it really *your* plans you're so concerned about?"

She frowned. "What do you mean?"

He raised his voice. "Don't you and God have this all planned out?" The vein in his neck pulsed. "You know, He gives you the inside scoop on the girl he wants your son to marry—a good Christian girl, of course— and you introduce us, we fall madly in love and get married. This is only possible, of course, if Brigit and I are no longer together and—"

"Now, don't get smart with me, Will."

He stood and pounded the table with his fist. "Well, am I right? You want me to marry a *Christian*."

She hesitated before answering. "Well, I suppose in a perfect world, I'd—"

"But, Mom, this isn't a perfect world. Right? That's why, according to you, we need a *savior*—to forgive our mistakes, change us, and guide us to the Great Hereafter." His heated sarcasm surprised even him.

"Will, we *all* need a savior. And, yes, He will guide us, if we let Him."

"So, what do we need God to save us *from*? To forgive us *for*?"

Her face flushed. "Our sins—the things we do wrong."

He slammed his open palm on the table. "Such as having a baby outside of marriage?"

"That's one thing. I believe God is willing to forgive *all* sins, including this pregnancy." She put her hand back on top of his. "Son, you've only known Brigit a couple of months. That means you'd just met her when this...happened."

Would it sound stupid if I told her I feel like I've known Brigit all of my life? "I didn't really know her. That's true. But I fell in love with her the moment I saw her." He brought his eyes up to meet hers. "I want to marry her someday, Mom."

"Love at first sight doesn't usually work out to be a real and lasting love. Brigit is a lovely girl, but don't compound this problem with an even bigger one by rushing into marriage. Please, please. Think long and hard about adoption. Down the road, if you still feel you love Brigit, then perhaps—"

Will jumped up from his seat and started up the stairs. "I'm going to bed, Mom. We have graduation rehearsal in the morning, and then I think I'll grab a newspaper and start my job search."

Her voice took on a soothing tone. "You're really serious about this, aren't you?"

He walked back down the steps to stand next to her at the table. "Of course. And Mom, you've got to understand one thing. If you and I are going to have a good relationship from now on—and I hope we can because we want you to be a part of our baby's life—you have to realize that Brigit and I are going to be in charge of our own lives, not God. I respect your beliefs. Now, please respect ours."

She nodded and bit her lower lip. "Just what *are* your beliefs? And whom are you going to go to for strength and guidance throughout your adult life? When you need comfort—"

Will's jaw grew tight and he shouted through gritted teeth. "Well, it's not going to be God, I can tell you that! He doesn't care about me.

Have you got that? He's never been there for me!" *He let Dad suffer. He let Dad die. He left me all alone!*

"That's not true, Will." She stood and placed a gentle hand on his back.

"Oh, yes it is. I prayed and prayed for God to heal Dad. I promised Him I'd do anything He wanted if He'd just let my father live. But He let Dad suffer, and then he took him away from us. And, don't forget how much *you* prayed. Why, you had the whole church praying and still he died. So, don't talk to me about answered prayer or healing or comfort."

"Will—"

"You can believe all that if you want to, but leave me out." He picked up the dishtowel and threw it into the center of the table next to the small ceramic container labeled, "Daily Bread," and bounded up the stairs. *I knew she wouldn't understand.*

———◆———

Will pointed his camera at Brigit, Sue and Mary Ellen. *Brigit looks so beautiful in her cap and gown. It's too bad they'll all be separated this next year, just when Brigit will need the support of her best friends the most.* "Say 'cheese'." The sharp *click* captured the historic moment for posterity.

"Hey, now the two of you." Mary Ellen took the camera from Will and snapped a picture of him and Brigit. "Perfect!" She handed the camera back to him. "Now, Sue and I have to go find our parents. We'll meet up with you later."

Sue turned and waved as they headed across the crowded football field. "Be sure to have a copy of those pictures made for us!"

Will removed his maroon robe, revealing a dampened shirt underneath. "It's so hot tonight and all of these stadium lights just make matters worse."

"I know, but you only graduate from college once. I'm keeping my robe on as long as possible." She pushed the long sleeves up and unzipped the front.

His mother, arms raised and waving, ran across the lawn strewn with folding chairs. "There you two are. I thought we were going to meet at the south goal post." His mother wiped her forehead with a tissue and removed her suit jacket. "This heat is unbearable!"

"That's Arizona for you!" Brigit forced a smile in her direction.

"Well, anyway. Congratulations to you both." She gave each of them a long hug. "I'm glad we took pictures before the ceremony. You both look like you just took a dip in a swimming pool." Her smile faded as she turned her attention to Brigit. "Will shared the news with me last night, Brigit, but made me promise not to ruin graduation for you by talking about it beforehand."

Will raised his eyebrows, squared his shoulders, and walked toward his mother.

"So why bring it up, now?"

Her face twitched. "Because I'd like the chance to talk to Brigit about the decision to keep the baby."

Brigit turned and glanced at him. Her voice trembled. "Will?"

He stepped between Brigit and his mother. "You don't have to do that. We make our own decisions. We have no one else to answer to but ourselves." He draped his arm around Brigit's shoulders and drew her close. *How dare she bring this up at graduation on the field with hundreds of people milling around. She never misses an opportunity...*

Brigit circumvented Will and walked toward his mother. "Our decision stands, Mrs. Hayes, but we'd welcome your support. I'd like nothing more than a loving grandmother for our baby." Brigit's eyes sparkled against the night sky.

His mother raised her eyebrows. "Grandmother? Let's not get ahead of ourselves. In my opinion, you need to consider all of your options before you—"

"Mom, this isn't the time or the place for this discussion. I told you that adoption isn't a consideration." He took Brigit by the arm and began to walk in the direction of the goal post where they'd planned to meet Brigit's parents. Over his shoulder, he called out to his mother as she stood, speechless, on the grassy lawn. "Be a grandmother or don't. That's the only decision *you* need to make."

CHAPTER 5

———————

Sᴡᴇᴀᴛ ᴛʀɪᴄᴋʟᴇᴅ ᴅᴏᴡɴ Wɪʟʟ'ꜱ ɴᴇᴄᴋ as he waited in the mid-morning heat for Derf to finish his racquetball game with Dan. He had put the top down on the Mustang and pulled it under the shade of a large Palo Verde tree at the far end of the parking lot. But the hula girl on the dash had a thermometer in her tummy and it already registered 100 degrees on this, the first official day of summer. He waved Derf over when he saw him leave the court.

"He whopped me, as usual." Derf plopped his gym bag and racquet into the back seat and slid into the one beside Will. "The car looks pretty sweet. You keep it spotless."

"It was Dad's baby. I just try to take care of it like he would have." He ran his hand along the top of the dash and brought it down to rest on the gearshift. "So, where would you like to eat?"

"Anywhere but The Chuckbox." Derf let out a hearty laugh.

Will chuckled, too. "Yeah. You've probably had your fill of burgers."

Derf's eyes lit up. "How about let's celebrate graduation and head for the lake?"

Will hesitated. "I'd sure like to, but I'd better not commit to a whole afternoon. I've got some job applications I want to drop off, and I'm meeting Brigit at five."

Will turned on the motor and the car sprang to life. "How about let's get a dog at Ted's?"

Derf licked his lips. "Sounds good."

Will pulled the car onto Apache Boulevard and headed east, enjoying the coolness of the air blowing through his damp hair. He nodded to the beat of the Beach Boys' newest release. *Why am I so nervous about telling Derf about the baby? I know I can count on his support. He's my best friend.*

Derf reached over and turned the radio down. "How's Brigit? I haven't seen her around for a while."

Will smiled, thinking of their plans to look for apartments later in the day. He'd like nothing better than sitting across from her at the dinner table each night. "Oh, she's fine. She's out job hunting, too."

"There are always openings in nursing. She shouldn't have a problem finding one right away." Derf narrowed his eyes. "But, hey, isn't she still planning on spending the summer with her folks?"

Will pulled into a parking space and hopped out of the car. He looked over his shoulder at Derf as he started up the tree-lined walkway toward Ted's Hot Dogs. "She was, but things have changed."

Derf caught up with him and they headed for the order window. "What things?"

"I'll explain over lunch. Why don't you put the order in and I'll snag that table over there. It's the only one with an umbrella." Will handed a five-dollar bill to Derf. "Be sure to get me a Dr. Pepper. All right?"

"Yep." Derf turned toward the freckle-faced teenage boy at the order window.

Will slid onto a bench seat and wiped catsup and breadcrumbs off the tabletop with a napkin. "A Hard Day's Night" played on the overhead speaker. *I don't need another lecture, or his advice—just some moral support.*

Derf placed a tall paper cup in front of Will. "Here's your drink. The dogs will be up in a few minutes. They're training a new guy. You know how *that* is." He sat down at the table facing Will.

Will sagged against the seat back. "I hope he's a fast learner. I'm starved."

Derf took a sip of his drink. "So, what changed Brigit's plans?"

Here goes. Will let out a long breath. "She's pregnant."

The soda from Derf's mouth sprayed across the table. "Wow. I didn't see that one coming."

"Me neither." Will wiped his t-shirt and face off with his napkin. *The truth is I never even gave the possibility of this happening the slightest thought at the time. I hope I'm more responsible as a parent than I've been as a boyfriend.*

Derf raised his eyebrows. "So it's not yours?"

Will rubbed his hand down his face. "Oh, it's mine. It's just that it surprised me, too. We were only together once." *Derf's had the same girlfriend for two years and she hasn't ended up pregnant. He must think I'm pretty stupid.*

Derf shook his head. "Bad timing, I suppose."

Will shrugged. "Yeah. I guess."

"Well, the last thing you need now is a lecture on abstinence or birth control."

"Yeah. I got that from my mother." Will rolled his eyes. He could still hear her angry words.

"I bet you did. She took it pretty hard, huh?"

"You could say that." Will sighed deeply. "She wants us to give it up for adoption."

Derf hesitated. He put his cup down and looked Will square in the eyes. "Maybe you should think about it."

"Not you, too!" Heat rushed through his body as he glared at his friend. He banged his clenched his fist on the table so hard that the his cup tipped over and the last of his soda spilled onto the table.

Derf stiffened. "Look, it might be for the best." He leaned forward and lowered his voice. "The baby gets a loving family, and you and Brigit get to know each other better before you—"

Will stood, placed both hands on the table, and leaned over the sticky mess. "You know what? I thought *you* might be supportive. I thought *you* might have some words of encouragement. But you sound more like a parent than a best friend."

Derf stood, placing his forehead against Will's. "Sorry. I guess I should have known to say only *what you want to hear* and not how I *really* feel." He backed off and sat back down. "But think about it, what kind of friend would I be if I didn't speak the truth?"

"Oh, no. This isn't going to turn out like our last conversation is it? The truth according to the newly-converted Christian who valiantly tries to lead his old friend to Christ." He curled his lip and mocked Derf. "Just be careful you don't turn into one of those Jesus freaks."

Derf sighed, calming his voice. "So maybe I *am* a little over-anxious for you to know God. It's just that since I went forward at that concert, I've felt like a new person. I want everyone to find what I've—"

Will raised his palm toward Derf. "You can just stop right there. I heard it all on the phone after the concert. Remember? And, I'm telling you for the last time that I don't see things the way you do." He took his seat again. "It doesn't make either one of us wrong. We're just going to have to agree to disagree and leave it at that. If you don't think that's possible, then I'll miss our friendship, but I'll understand." *Dad wasn't duped by all of this "God has a plan for your life" talk and I'm not going to be either.*

Derf slumped back against his seat. He looked up at Will with pleading eyes. "You can't stop me praying for you and Brigit and the baby."

"No, and I won't even try. But, Brigit and I want to live our life *our* way. We need you to accept that or I'm afraid you should find a new best friend."

———◆———

Brigit sipped on an Orange Julius as she waited for Will inside the food court at Fiesta Mall. She was fifteen minutes early, but she'd been shopping for maternity clothes for an hour, and it felt good to sit down. Anyway, she was hungry again. She wondered if the growing baby could be making her want to eat so often. She reached into her shoulder bag and pulled out the copy of *Parents Magazine* that Sue and Mary Ellen had given her before they left. She thumbed through the pages of illustrations. *Let's see, twelve weeks... Not very big yet, are you my baby?*

Brigit rubbed her belly. She wasn't showing yet, but she could hardly wait. Somehow that would make the whole pregnancy seem more real. She didn't yet need the maternity clothes she had bought this afternoon, but her mother had sent her a cheerful card and some money in yesterday's mail. She wrote that she wanted Brigit to buy herself some clothes with it, knowing that the baby would take priority soon enough.

Brigit pulled a small white teddy bear out of the shopping bag. She held it up to her cheek and closed her eyes, imagining how she would snuggle with her newborn. *I love you already, little one. You give me such happiness and purpose. I promise to be the best mom for you that I can possibly be. You will have a mother and father that will love you above all else. We will protect you always.*

She wished her parents hadn't moved to Indiana, although her mother had told her that she'd come and stay with them for a while once the baby was born. In the meantime she was halfway across the country, and her best friends were noticeably absent. That left her no one but Will for moral support. *Sue said most guys would feel trapped, but Will doesn't seem to feel that way. He's wonderful. But how can I be sure he'll be here for me in the long run?* She wrinkled her nose. *Could Sue be right about this?*

There was no valid reason for her to think Will would bail on her and the baby. After all, he was postponing grad school and getting a job. That should be proof enough that he loved her and would stand beside her. There was no rationale for her worrying like this. Still…

"Is this seat taken, miss?" Will kissed her on top of the head and then swung into the seat across from her. "I see you're drinking healthy."

She forced a smile hoping that her dark thoughts hadn't lingered in her eyes. "I am. Do you want one?"

He rubbed his stomach. "Maybe later. I'm still full from lunch." He picked up the book and thumbed through it before placing it back onto the table. "Doing some heavy-duty reading, too, I see."

"It's a magazine Sue and Mary Ellen gave me. Very informative." She blushed and placed it back inside her bag. "How did your talk with Derf go?"

He shook his head. "Not so well. I'm just now calming down."

Brigit placed her hand on his. "What happened?"

"He was surprised, to put it mildly. I think he kind of agreed with Mom about adoption."

Her eyes widened. Derf seemed so easy going, she was surprised he had even voiced an opinion. Did Christianity change people that much? "R-r-really?" she stammered, her brows knitting together and forming a frown.

"Yeah. But, I told him we were getting jobs and want to raise our baby. I told him that *we* get to make the decisions about our own life, not them. And, I gave him the same choice I gave Mom: be supportive or leave us alone. We don't need their lectures on God. We don't need God. Period."

In theory, she agreed with him. But when it came right down to it, would the two of them be able to make it on their own? It was one thing to get to make their own decisions, but quite another to put forth the hard work and effort necessary to advance their careers and maintain a growing family. It would be difficult without the help of family and friends.

Derf said God has a plan for every life. Did that mean their baby was a part of His plan and not the "big mistake" that sometimes nagged at her thoughts? If so, she could now embrace the growing baby inside her. She could love her baby without reservation. And, if one day Will would decide that this wasn't the life that *he* wanted and *he* planned for, then she and the baby would just have to make it on their own.

Could Brigit and Will's unplanned baby actually have been planned by God? Did that make sense? Or was she only just grasping at straws—trying to hang onto anything that might purge her own guilty feelings?

———

After a picnic lunch at Daley Park, Will compared his first paycheck with Brigit's. "I can't believe how much money they took out for taxes and insurance. Can you?" He'd have to be frugal, once they moved in together, if they were really going to be able to make it on their own.

Brigit shook her head as she stared at the pay stub from the community hospital. "I know my parents used to complain about that, but I honestly didn't pay any attention."

He added their take home amounts to the list on his legal pad. "Are you ready for our three-month grand total?" He raised his eyebrows and displayed a mischievous grin.

"I guess so. " She took in a long breath and let it out. "I just hope we have enough for our first and last months' rent. I'd hate for them to rent the apartment to someone else."

He gave a long drum roll on the tabletop. "And, the total is $1,600!"

She reached over to kiss his lips. "Woo hoo! We did it!"

Will put aside the legal pad. "With my continuing to live at home, we've managed to save most of what we've made. But after we move into our own place, the only way we can keep afloat is to stick to our budget—no matter what. If there's a little money left over at the end of the month, we can splurge on a gourmet meal at McDonald's. What do you say?" He traced a path from her elbow down to her wrist with his forefinger.

She flashed a big smile and snuggled close. "I agree. And I'm glad we're getting the one bedroom apartment. The bigger one would have been far too expensive. When the baby gets older, we can move some-where with more room. But for now, he'll just have to bunk with us."

He shrugged. "It's an older building, though. That means the pos-sibility of maintenance problems."

"I know I was all set on something new, but at least it's been freshly painted and the furniture that comes with it isn't really so bad. All we need now is a crib." She slipped a furniture store flyer out of her purse and pushed it across the table toward him. "This store is having a sale next weekend." She raised her eyebrows. "What do you think?"

He picked it up and came around to sit on the bench beside her. He thumbed through the pages. "These are awfully expensive." He put his arm around her and gave her a gentle squeeze. "Maybe it would be fun to find a used one and refinish it ourselves. I've done a few projects with Mom and they turned out okay. In fact, you know that sideboard in the dining room? We refinished that one. The key is in the sanding. If we do a good job of that, we'll have a beautiful crib for little Max."

Brigit looked up at him and smiled. "Max, huh? What if the baby's a girl?"

He raised his eyebrows. "Maxine?"

She broke into laughter. "Maybe we should consult that book I bought you. There are probably some names in there we might want to consider."

He slipped her hand into his. "Did you realize that this coming Monday would have been our first day of graduate school?"

She shook her head. "Wow! The summer went fast, didn't it?" She smoothed her maternity blouse over her growing belly.

"Yeah." He used his forefinger to tip her chin toward him. "Are you disappointed not to be starting your P.A. training?"

She shrugged. "Not really. I mean it *is* something I want to do later on. But for now I'm enjoying being in the delivery room. It's kinda like on the job training, if you know what I mean."

He heaved a sigh of relief. "I don't regret not being in grad school, either. I'm happy being a reporter, and I think I'll be able to work my way up without another degree. I'm up for a pay review in another three months. I'll work hard to get it, too. The extra money will really help out." If he started saving for Graduate School now, he'd have enough in a few years in case he changed his mind and resurrected his abandoned dreams.

"I'm just glad we got jobs right away so we could save for our apartment. I know your living at home has been a strain on both you and your Mom. I was fortunate that Sue and Mary Ellen let me share their rental. All summer. Rent-free. I don't know what I would have done otherwise." She snuggled close and rested her head on his shoulder.

His fingers played with a stray curl that had fallen in front of her face. *If she only knew how hard it's really been. I know Mom means well. She's been better than I expected, given our differences of opinion. Still, I'll be relieved not to have to listen to her barrage of Bible verses for every situation that comes up.* "If Mom had let you stay with us—"

She kicked off her sandals and pushed her toes into the thick grass. "I know. But we have to respect her decision. She doesn't want us moving in together because she feels it isn't morally right to live together without being married."

"But regardless of what she thinks, we're moving in one week from today." He grinned, kissed her gently on the cheek, then pulled back to look into her eyes. "It's not too late to back out, if you want to."

"Nope. Food or no food, bed or no bed, you're stuck with me." She gave his hand a quick squeeze. "What about you? Getting cold feet?

"Not in the least. If you don't steal the covers while we sleep, I'll be a happy man."

CHAPTER 6

———•———

INHALING THE FRAGRANCE OF HER perfume, Will planted gentle kisses on
Brigit's neck and shoulders. At nearly six months pregnant, her figure
had definitely changed, but that didn't matter to him. She was still the
most gorgeous girl on earth.

Once they had finished unloading the car and hung the last of their
clothing in the small bedroom closet, it was almost two o'clock. Brigit
looked exhausted, so he threw one of Grandma Hayes's quilts over the
unmade bed and convinced her to lie down with him to rest.

While she slept, he lay awake. He was tired, but couldn't possibly
sleep. He looked forward to the late afternoon sun dipping beyond the
horizon of slump block apartments and the beginning of their first evening in their own place. It wasn't much. Just four rooms—four very small
rooms: a bedroom, bathroom, kitchen, and living area—but it was theirs.

Tomorrow they would unpack the pillows and pictures his mother
had given them to make their space look more colorful and inviting.
He'd put away the Melmac dishes, Teflon skillet and half-dozen mixed-
matched glasses they'd purchased from the garage sale down the street.
Then they'd take a leisurely walk around the block to orient themselves to the new neighborhood.

He smoothed the quilt, his forefinger tracing the stitches securing an
odd-shaped patch. He thought about the Christmas that his grandmother

had given it to him. Like any nine-year-old, he had been expecting a toy. When he unwrapped her gift, he'd been disappointed. He still remembered her wistful look as she held both of his hands in hers and told him the story of the quilt, the patchwork symbolizing the love of family.

The denim pieces were from Grandpa's old overalls. He was a farmer, and Will couldn't remember a time when he wore anything other than the baggy attire, one strap always flapping in the wind. The pink and yellow flowered material had been saved from Great Grandma Hayes's apron. She had loved to cook. The worn and stained fabric held fond memories of good times around his grandparents' table.

There were other mementos sewn in place, too. His favorite was an old red handkerchief that Grandpa had tied as a tourniquet around Will's leg when he fell off the hay baler and landed on a pitchfork. Grandpa's face had drained of all color as he scooped him up in his arms and placed him in the bed of the truck. The usual drive time into town was twenty minutes. Gramps had made it in ten.

Will read the familiar words on the small white patch in the quilt's corner: "To my Grandson, Will. This quilt represents the intertwining of lives brought together by the divine wisdom of God, and stitched with love and prayers by your grandmother, Helene Hayes. December 25, 1967."

He slid off the bed, watching the rise and fall of Brigit's back as she slept. He thought of the day they had met, their picnic at the lake, and the love that had brought them to the sixth month of Brigit's pregnancy. Their lives had intertwined, too, but he was sure it wasn't God that had brought them together.

It was fate. Some might have even called it destiny. He shook his head. No, something this special could never have come from the same God that turned a deaf ear to his own desperate prayers to spare the life of his father.

He walked into the small bathroom. There was barely enough space for him to turn around. The paint was peeling around the window and next to the sink. On the walls, faded decals of starfish and seashells were still visible underneath the new coat of paint when the sunlight hit them at just the right angle.

He put one of the new washcloths under the faucet, wrung it out almost dry, and ran it over his face and arms. He stared at the brown and white striped washcloth as he hung it over the side of the claw foot tub. Derf had come around. Not only had he helped them move, but he also presented them with the set of towels as a housewarming gift. Will suspected they were actually more of a peace offering.

He was glad to have his best friend back. Even though he and Brigit were together almost every day all summer long, it just wasn't the same as having a guy friend. He had missed hanging out, shooting hoops, and eating at The Chuckbox. He was eager to know what had happened between Derf and his girlfriend to change his mind about moving in together as they had planned. He was sure it was just another casualty due to Derf's obsession with God and Christianity.

———◆———

The last three months of Brigit's pregnancy flew by. There was a lot to do to prepare for the baby. The refinishing of the hand-me-down crib that was given to her from Sue's older sister, Marilyn, turned out to be more Will's project than one for the both of them. He had allowed her to help with the sanding, but the rest of the work he'd done by himself. He hadn't wanted Brigit to breathe the fumes from the paint and possibly harm the baby.

Now, with only days to go, Brigit and Will sat at opposite ends of the old red-and-green plaid sofa. He picked up her right foot and began to massage it. Her ankles were swollen from being on her feet so much the last few months. One of the nurses on her floor had quit and she often took on an extra shift. Will didn't want her to work herself to the point of exhaustion, but she knew they could use the additional income.

Will worked on breaking news stories all around the state, so he was often away from home a few days at a time. When he was gone, and she didn't have the energy to fix dinner for herself, she either skipped the meal or ate at the hospital cafeteria. She sometimes worried about her health—and the baby's—but she kept her concerns to herself. After all, Will was big on nutrition and wouldn't want to hear that she didn't always eat properly.

When he was home, Will did most of the cooking and cleaning. She felt guilty that he didn't have any time left over to see any of his friends. If he began to see their life together as only dishes and diapers, he might never want to get married.

She often fantasized about what it might be like to have him ask her to marry him, but she had only hinted at the subject once. And, since he hadn't taken the bait, she had just let the matter drop. She knew him by now. He would want the moment to be special. At this point, the baby's birth was enough for both of them to focus on.

She watched through the screen door as the sky turned a brilliant orange and then faded into darkness. When it was impossible for them to see each other any longer, she reached behind her to turn on the lamp.

Will let out a contented sigh and smiled at her in the same endearing way she had come to adore. "Any day now, the baby should be here. According to the book, your 'nesting instinct' should kick in a few days before the baby comes. All of a sudden, you'll get a burst of energy and start cleaning and—"

"Well, I sure wish I had some of it now. I worry that I won't be able to take care of the baby and keep up with the apartment when you're out of town." Her eyes filled with tears and she hurried to wipe them away.

He placed her foot on the sofa and moved down to sit beside her, kissing her tenderly. "Of course you will. It's the long hours you've been working that have made you so tired. We've saved up enough so you can take a whole month off and just enjoy the baby. Let everything else go. Your bag is all packed and ready. It's all under control."

Maybe everything seemed to be under control to him. He wasn't the one who was soon to give birth. She'd seen a few complicated births in the short time that she'd been working at the hospital. She'd heard the horror stories. Would hers be one of them? Her voice wasn't much more than a whisper. "I'm scared."

"Don't be. You'll be a fantastic mom." He placed the fluffy slippers back on her feet. "I'm done here, so why don't you take a nice warm bath while I make us some mac and cheese? I'll add some of that left-over broccoli. Then after we eat, we'll turn in early and get a good night's rest." He helped her up from the sofa.

She felt like he hadn't really heard her concerns. Like he'd dismissed her feelings. His words were encouraging, but... She guessed she'd just keep her fears to herself. She didn't want Will to think she was weak. Millions of women before her had gone through labor and delivery. She'd put on a happy face and maybe he'd forget she'd even said that much.

She pasted a smile on her face. "That sounds good. Tomorrow's Saturday, and after we do a little laundry and housecleaning, we can lay around for the rest of the weekend if we want." She gave him a quick peck on the cheek, followed by a yawn and a stretch.

"If you're a good girl, I may even bring you breakfast in bed." He guided her shoulders toward the bathroom. "Leave the door open and I'll help you out of the tub when you're done with your bath."

As she padded down the hall, she felt the sudden need to tell him everything. She turned back toward him, taking a half-dozen steps to close the gap between them. "Will?"

"Yes?"

She hesitated. Maybe she was just being silly. She shouldn't misinterpret her building apprehension for anything more than what it was—the natural fears any young mother would have about childbirth. "Thanks for the foot massage. You're amazing!"

"You're welcome. You've got twenty minutes, so scoot and let the chef whip up a culinary masterpiece." He turned toward the small kitchen with the flickering overhead light and worn linoleum floor.

She headed to the bathroom. Her hand shook as she turned the faucet handle to the right and stepped into the tub. She eased herself down into the warm water, laid her head back against the vinyl bath pillow, and closed her eyes.

Her thoughts went to her phone conversation a few weeks earlier with Mary Ellen. Could she have possibly been right about Will? Brigit had defended him to her friend, but now the seed of doubt that Mary Ellen had planted was taking root in her heart.

Her friend had certainly been forthright in her assessment of Brigit's relationship with Will. "I'm not saying this to hurt you, but it's too soon for guys like Will. If it weren't for the baby, he'd be off at grad school, playing the field, reveling in the attention the good-looking jocks always get. As much as you'd like to think it isn't so, he needs to get everything out of his system. He's just not ready to settle down."

"You don't know him. He's different." Brigit had protested, looking down at her growing belly.

"I'm telling you that this baby cements your relationship right now. Will may try to be a stand-up guy, but when the going gets tough and he has to spend money on diapers and doctor bills instead of beer and pizza, he'll leave you and the baby behind. You'll be lucky if he takes the kid for weekend visits. The cement will crumble. Years from now, he'll settle down and have his 'forever family' with someone who is there at the *right time* and the *right place*."

Brigit needed support from her friend. Why couldn't Mary Ellen encourage her a little...say some kind words? She recalled the time she'd cut her own comment short in order to make Mary Ellen feel better after her abortion. If anyone knew just how fragile a pregnant woman's feelings could be, it should be Mary Ellen.

The sound of Will's voice down the hall brought Brigit back to the present reality of a mac and cheese dinner made in a kitchen with a two-burner stove and eaten on TV trays in front of a blank wall where a television ought to sit. She wiped escaping tears from her face and lifted herself out of the water. She grasped the side of the tub to steady herself, stepping onto the fluffiness of the new bathmat.

"Hey, supper's getting cold. Let me help you—"

Brigit was dabbing at her eyes with the edge of her towel when Will pushed back the half-open door.

"Sweetie, what's the matter? Have you been crying?" His jaw dropped open, his eyes riveted on something near her feet.

Puzzled, she cocked her head to the side. Her eyes followed his gaze downward to the thin line of blood trickling down the inside of her leg.

———————

Will glanced at the road, then to Brigit, and back to the road again. It was two weeks before her due date. The book had said first babies were often late, but he guessed books couldn't possibly know everything about each individual situation. This baby—their baby—was coming early.

He had read something in Brigit's book about blood, but couldn't remember the details. It wasn't necessarily a bad sign was it? Except for working so hard, Brigit had been so careful. She hadn't fallen or drunk alcohol. Why, then, did he have this uneasy feeling?

He worried about her going through the pain of labor. He had heard so many stories over the past months. He was glad, as a guy, he'd never have to feel that kind of pain. Yet seeing the fear in her eyes as he had eased her into the backseat of the Mustang, he immediately felt guilty for having such thoughts. He hoped that by the time they got to the hospital, she'd reconsider her vow to have natural childbirth and take the painkilling drugs if she needed them.

They had completed all of their Lamaze classes last week. One out of the four couples that had been in the same class with them had already given birth to a girl. When Brigit had heard the news, she had insisted they leave dinner on the table and rush to the hospital to see the baby. From the many questions Brigit had asked, however, he realized she was more interested in hearing about Trudy's birth experience than in welcoming the baby.

All of a sudden, he put two-and-two together. *Brigit is afraid!* He had thought that earlier, when she said she was scared, she meant she was apprehensive about the many responsibilities of being a mother. But now he realized that she had been talking about giving birth. *What an unfeeling, self-centered person she must think I am!* He had unknowingly dismissed her feelings when she needed his support the most.

Like a doctor that tells his patient to take two aspirin and call him in the morning, Will had told her that a warm bath and a plate of mac and cheese was all she needed. In reality, she needed *him*. He'd just been too dense to realize it.

"Ahhh!" she moaned. She closed her eyes and started to breathe in slow, controlled breaths, just the way she had learned in class.

Will glanced back and forth between Brigit in the rear view mirror and the road ahead. "You're doing great. We're almost there. After the bridge, it's a straight shot for the last mile." He used his forearm to wipe away the sweat from his forehead.

"It hurts so—bad! I can't do it, Will!"

Will kissed two fingers and reached back over the seat to place them on Brigit's trembling lips. "Just think. You'll be holding our little baby in your arms in just a few more minutes. Breathe with me next time you get a contraction, okay?"

"I want my mom!"

Will could hear the desperation in her voice. "When I get you all settled, I'll give your parents a call." He pressed on the accelerator as he entered the divided highway.

"Hurry, Will. I—can't —"

"I'm speeding as it is, Brig. I'm doing the best I can." As the car passed under a streetlight, he gasped. *Too much blood. Definitely, too much blood.*

The Mustang screeched to a halt next to the emergency doors. Two men in blue scrubs ran out to the car and opened the door. One ran back for a gurney, and Will and the other man gently lifted Brigit out and cradled her until it arrived.

"Will, I can't take it. Ahhh—the pain is constant!"

Brigit's face was pale and her hand was sweaty as she clenched onto Will. Her fingernails dug into the palm of his hand as he walked beside her, past the nurses' station, and straight through the door labeled "Labor and Delivery." He wouldn't leave her side. He'd calm himself down and remember what he'd learned in class. He'd be the support she needed to get through this. Now was the time to prove to her just how much he cared—just how much he was committed to their relationship. Just how much he loved her.

The shorter of the two men held out his arm, pushing against Will's chest and backing him out of the room. "You can't be in here without scrubs. From the looks of things, maybe not at all."

Will raised his eyebrows and let out a ragged breath. "You don't understand. We took Lamaze classes. Just show me where to get my scrubs and I'll be in there in a few minutes."

"Mr.?"

"Hayes. Will."

"Well, Will, let us get your wife settled and you go get her admitted at the desk we passed down the hall. We'll come get you if the doctor approves it, okay?"

Not okay. Definitely not okay. "I don't want to leave her—Brigit—she's afraid and—"

Two nurses scurried past them and into the delivery room. They were followed a moment later by a doctor, tall and thin with his mask hanging around his neck.

"Got to go. I'll come talk to you once the doctor looks her over. Everything will be fine."

"But—"

"She's in good hands, really. Now, go." He held the door open for another nurse as she rolled an incubator inside.

Will caught a glimpse of Brigit, her frightened eyes following him as he stood helplessly frozen to the spot.

"Will!" She raised up on one arm and reached out for him with the other.

The door clicked shut.

Will pounded on the door's frosted glass panel. "Brigit!" He felt light headed. He slid down to the floor and rested his head on his bent knees. He took a deep breath and shuddered. Nothing was happening as the instructor had described. He'd known something was very wrong the moment he'd seen all that blood...

He might be able to get one of Brigit's co-workers to find out what was happening. He paced back and forth in front of the nurse's station, waiting for one of them to show up.

He had called his mother. Even though she had assured him that she was on the way, his heart still pounded. He gagged as he tasted a foul liquid in his mouth. Sometime tonight he would be a father. That awesome responsibility hit him, and added to the apprehension that had been building over the past two hours. His legs turned to jelly.

He collapsed onto the cushioned bench in the waiting room, putting his elbows on his knees and cradling his head in his hands. *What was taking so long?*

Dad had been in this very hospital when he died. By the time Will had been allowed into the room, he had already turned pale. The same ghostly white of Brigit's face nearly two hours ago... *Please, no!* He shook his head to clear it. He couldn't let his mind go there.

The wide hall, once bustling with activity, was now eerily quiet. It was almost midnight. He looked back at the doors to the delivery room. They were still closed. He walked over to the water fountain and took a long drink, then crossed the room to look through the window overlooking the parking lot. He ran his fingers through his hair. Where could his mother be?

The lights of an oncoming car cast shadows onto the asphalt. He sighed as he recognized his mother's white Oldsmobile pull into the space beside his Mustang.

Hitting the square metal button on the wall, he squeezed through the still-opening doors and ran down the sidewalk. He jumped over the flowering shrubs that lined the grassy landscape, grabbed the shiny handle, and pulled the car door open. "Mom, thanks for—" His jaw dropped and he stumbled back as first his mother, and then four of her lady friends, tumbled out.

CHAPTER 7

———◆———

STILLBORN.

Had he heard the doctor right? Will sank to his knees on the cold tile floor of the hospital waiting room, unable to catch his breath. The surprise pregnancy, the months that he and Brigit had both worked two jobs, the disapproval unleashed by his mother—is this the way it would end?

His mother crossed the room and put her hand on his shoulder. She cleared her throat. "Son, I am so sorry. Truly, I am."

Heat coursed throughout his body. He glared at her as he slowly rose to his feet. "Come on, this is what you were hoping for all along! I bet you even *prayed* for this to happen."

She hung her head as he hurled insult after insult.

This would be a relief for her. The illegitimate child would no longer be a constant reminder to her of her son's sin. "This all works out for you so well, doesn't it, Mom?"

"You can't really think that I would take pleasure in your misery." Her voice trembled. Sobbing, she buried her head in her hands. "I'd never pray for something like this to happen. I—"

"You know, why don't you just get out? We don't need you here. We don't *want* you here." The words escaped through his gritted teeth.

"And take your little prayer partners with you." He nodded in the direction of the four ladies huddled in the corner, eyes closed and heads bent in prayer.

Black mascara ran down her cheeks. "Will—"

"I mean it, Mother. I thought you'd be supportive, but I've spent the last two hours alone while you prayed with *them*." His hands shook as he pointed to her friends, sitting across the room with tear-streaked faces. "And, just like with Dad, God didn't choose to save a life. So just leave me alone while I think of what to say to Brigit when she gets settled in a room. Can you do that?"

The slow clicks of his mother's heels, followed by hushed voices and more shuffling of feet, preceded the sharp blast of cold winter air from the opening and closing of the sliding glass door.

Our baby never even took his first breath. He massaged the back of his neck, and then turned his face toward the hallway leading to the Labor and Delivery wing at Tempe Community Hospital.

A compassionate God wouldn't have allowed this to happen. A caring God wouldn't have destroyed what they'd created in love. Or, on second thought, maybe he had—in retaliation for their lack of faith. God let their baby die. The money they saved to provide for it would now be spent on a casket and a funeral.

Will slumped into a nearby vinyl chair. His heartbeat increased as a vision of his little boy laughing and playing in the tall green grass outside their meager apartment gave way to a new reality: a coffin with a still, tiny form nestled inside.

He snatched a magazine and threw it against the wall. He grabbed another, then another, throwing dozens of them in all directions until all that remained on the table was a lone statue of a cherub. The smile on its face and its outstretched wings only fueled his anger. His hand swept across the table's smooth surface in a single movement, sending it full force against the floor. *Why, God, why?*

———◆———

Brigit refused to talk, so Will drove in silence the entire five miles from the hospital to their home. He tucked her into bed, drawing the quilt over her shoulders and kissed her forehead.

Her closed eyes told him what her lips would not: she didn't want to let him in. She didn't want share her grief with him. They had always told each other everything. Why wouldn't she talk to him now? He ached for just a word…a look…some acknowledgement that she knew he was hurting, too…that he mattered.

He looked down at the soft ringlets strewn across her pillow. If he didn't know otherwise, he'd think this was a poignant scene straight from a box office hit. The camera would pan over to the small suitcase. It had been packed with care for their baby's arrival, but now it was nothing more than a grim reminder of their grief—abandoned in the corner of the dingy bedroom.

So much had happened in the last few days.

He closed the door and began to pace across the thinly-carpeted living room. He waited for her to call for him. He needed her—they needed each other—to get through this.

When he heard a knock on the front door, he pulled back the pleated curtains and looked outside. He sighed with relief when it wasn't his mother, as he had expected. Instead it was the neighbor from across the street, the late afternoon sun shining through his thinning hair. Will had seen him a few times in the past couple of weeks as he pulled in and out of his garage, waving and smiling as if they were the best of friends. He shook his head. He didn't even know the guy's name.

Another somewhat louder knock followed the first. The guy sure was persistent. He had a covered dish in his hands. Was he selling something?

Will was in no mood to have someone expound on the many uses of Tupperware, but if he didn't answer soon, the guy would wake up Brigit. He flung the door open.

"Yeah. What can I do for you?" His voice was edgy and abrupt. He rested his bent elbow against the doorframe, his other hand on his waist.

"I'm Jim, your neighbor from across the street. My wife made you a casserole. We heard your wife had been in the hospital and thought she might not be up to cooking, yet." He placed the warm dish into Will's hands with a half-smile. "Hope you enjoy it. It's my favorite: a spicy version of macaroni and cheese. Kelley figured everybody likes it. She always says, 'You can't go wrong with mac and cheese.' She—"

Will slammed the door shut, drowning out the rest of Jim's dribble. He walked stiff-legged to the kitchen and placed the dish inside the refrigerator. Besides a few condiments in the door, it was the only thing on the wire shelf. Maybe he'd reheat it for himself and Brigit after she woke up. It looked like it would be that or nothing.

He would watch some television to pass the time—that is, if they had a television. He sat down on the sofa, picked up the small stack of mail from the coffee table and thumbed through it. There was an electric bill, water bill, and an invitation to Christmas services at the new church down the road. He tore the postcard in half and in half again, letting the pieces of colored paper flutter to the floor. He leaned forward and placed his head in his hands. His entire body shook as the tears he'd kept at bay for the last ninety-six hours came all at once.

Brigit rummaged through the only drawer in the small bathroom, looking for the package of razor blades she had unpacked months ago. Her heart quickened as her fingers came into contact with the hard plastic case.

She tore it open, dropped a single blade onto her open palm, and then brought it to eye level. It glistened in the sunlight filtering through the glass window. It was almost...beautiful... offering relief from the constant thoughts that plagued her—ugly, dark thoughts surrounding the birth...the moments waiting for the cry that never came. She swallowed a moan and glanced at the door. Holding her breath, she waited for Will to march in. She shook her head and relaxed her shoulders.

Red, swollen eyes stared back at her in the mirror. Gaunt and pale, she looked nothing like the vivacious young woman that had won Will's heart last spring. Her life had seemed magical at the time, but she now found it impossible to recall those feelings. The hopes and dreams she had for the future had blown away like the leaves on the tree outside their bedroom window, its branches bare and fruitless.

Her hands trembled as she fumbled with the lid on the bottle of pain pills. Six left. She took them all, allowing the empty bottle to *clatter* onto the floor. She once read that most people who overdosed on pills could be saved if found in time. She couldn't take that chance. But the razor blade was sharp. Clean. One swift motion would bring the sweet release she longed for.

She walked from bathroom toward the softness of the area rug and slid down to the floor. She propped her back against the foot of the bed and laid her head onto the mattress. When she was a child, she loved to lay on a quilt with her mother and take an afternoon nap under the large Palo Verde tree in their backyard. Before drifting off, they would look at the clouds, imagining them to look like faces or familiar objects. She closed her eyes, visualizing herself riding on a cirrus cloud, lulled to sleep as a gentle breeze rocked it back and forth in a pale blue sky.

As her eyes grew heavy and her breathing slowed, she raised the blade to her left wrist. She winced. It was just as she imagined. She closed her eyes. This would be the last pain she would ever feel, no longer a slave to thoughts of inadequacy, failure, shame, and loneliness. In a few moments, she would be reunited with her baby boy. She smiled. "Shh. Mommy's coming..."

———◆———

It was dark when he woke up. He shivered in the cold as he pulled himself upright on the edge of the sofa. How long had he been asleep? At least a couple of hours, because it had been daylight when Jim left. He switched on the pole lamp.

He walked over to the thermostat. Seventy degrees. He ran the dial up to seventy-four. He stumbled to the bedroom door and knocked softly. His stomach growled as he waited for Brigit to answer. She should be awake by now, and hungry, too. Maybe he shouldn't have been so rude to Jim. After all, he had brought them dinner.

He turned the knob and slowly entered the darkened room. "Brig? Time to wake up." He slipped on something wet on the concrete floor and caught hold of the dresser's edge to break his fall. *What in the world?* He fumbled for the wall switch and turned on the overhead light.

Brigit was lying on the floor in a pool of blood, her face pale.

"No! Sweetheart. Not you, too!" He trembled as he knelt to cradle her limp body. His tears dampened her hair as he rocked back and forth. His heart raced as his shaking hands ran over her body, looking for the source of the blood. He froze when he saw the gaping wound on her wrist. He pulled a handkerchief out of a nearby laundry basket and tied it around the injury to stop the flow.

He ran to the kitchen and grabbed the telephone receiver from the wall. Icy shivers traveled down his spine. He searched the emergency numbers posted on the refrigerator. Where was it? Where was it? Ah, there. His fingers fumbled as he dialed for an ambulance. *Please don't die. We still have each other! I need you!*

CHAPTER 8

———•———

BACK IN THE HOSPITAL, BRIGIT drifted in and out of sleep the next several days. Every time she awoke, she saw Will in rumpled clothes, sleeping in the chair by her bed. She knew he wanted to talk, but she just couldn't. Whenever he approached her, she'd roll over and face the white, sterile hospital wall.

Didn't he understand that she didn't want to live? How could she exist without her baby? She knew Will loved her, but she didn't have anything to give in return—at least not now. Seeing him only made her feel guilty.

Her escaping tears soaked the pillow. *Had she done something wrong that caused the baby to die? Did Will blame her? Would Mary Ellen's prediction come true?*

She hadn't wanted to see Sue, Mary Ellen, or even her own parents who flew to Phoenix to comfort her. But she especially didn't want to see Will. She was glad the chaplain came to visit when he wasn't there. She was sure his reaction to Rev. Walker's bedside prayer wouldn't have been pleasant. She bit her lip.

She reached under her pillow to pull out the New Testament Rev. Walker had given her. She opened it to the place marked with his business card, Revelation 21:4 "He will wipe every tear from their eyes.

There will be no more death or mourning or crying or pain." She could only imagine what that would be like. She wanted it so desperately.

She left the hospital two weeks later. She was thankful that Will had already returned to work so she could sleep the days and nights away, trying not to think about the baby…not feeling guilty that she wasn't spending time with Will and going on with life as if nothing had happened.

Will said they should name their baby, but she felt that if they gave him a name, he'd be more real to them than ever. A name would give him a permanent place in her heart when what she really wanted was to let their plans for his future just fade from her memory…

She slid her feet into her slippers and walked over to the bedroom window. Even in Arizona, the winters got cold. The heater ran constantly.

She pulled back the curtains, her eyes squinting in the morning sunlight. Children were playing in the yard across the street. A young woman with red hair, slightly older than herself, held a towheaded toddler. *Could all four of those kids possibly be hers?* And here she was with no baby to hold. Her arms ached. She blinked back the sudden rush of tears and let the curtains fall back into place.

After washing her face with warm water, she ventured to the kitchen. The garbage was overflowing, the sink stacked high with dishes, and the casserole of half-eaten mac and cheese the neighbor had brought was green, crusty, and still sitting in the middle of the table.

She opened the door and set the smelly garbage can outside. The sudden cold assaulted her face. As she shut the door, the calendar on the wall caught her attention. The last page had been turned. No longer was a turkey strutting in a barnyard. The picture had been replaced with one of children opening Christmas gifts. That could have been their family by this time next year. That would never happen, now. She ripped off the page and let it fall to the floor. She couldn't believe it was already December. She had somehow missed Thanksgiving.

Her mother's words echoed through her head from yesterday's phone call. "Honey, life must go on. I know this isn't what you want to hear, but you have to make an effort. Get up every day. Get dressed. Eat a good breakfast. Then, do something meaningful to keep your mind off what happened. When you do, one day you'll realize things *are* better, again. Please try, honey. If you won't do it for yourself—or Will—would you do it for me? I'm so far away and I worry about you."

Brigit had made a half-hearted promise to her mother. If that was what she wanted, she would go through the motions. She'd paste on a smile and pretend life had meaning and purpose. She yanked off her nightgown and picked up a sweatshirt from a pile of laundry in the living room rocker. Sniffing it, she guessed Will had gone to the laundromat, but just hadn't bothered to fold anything. She wouldn't complain. It was more than she had done.

She pulled the sweatshirt over her head, shook out a wrinkled pair of jeans and slipped them on, too. She washed the casserole dish and dried it. She'd take it back to her neighbor, apologizing that she'd taken so long to return it. She grabbed a jacket and opened the door. The fresh air felt good.

———◆———

Brigit couldn't remember the last time she'd laughed. Her neighbor Kelley's funny stories were just what she needed to lift her spirits. She had to admit, Mom had been right, like always.

She accepted Kelley's invitation to stay for lunch. It seemed so natural to eat bologna and cheese sandwiches with Kelley and her kids, as if they were old friends just catching up.

The afternoon passed quickly. They talked on Kelley's covered front porch while her kids rode their bicycles up and down the sidewalk.

Brigit smiled as Karen, Kelley's youngest, played "Peek-a-Boo" with her. She found herself enjoying the game as much as the little girl seemed to, both giggling and laughing until Karen snuggled into her mother's lap and fell asleep. "I hope I'll have children who are just as handsome and well-behaved as yours."

"So, are you thinking of starting a family, soon?" Kelley's eyes crinkled around the edges when she smiled.

Brigit's head spun. All of a sudden she was spiraling down the familiar rabbit hole. Dark thoughts pounced at her, threatening to regain control of her life. She squeezed her eyes shut, struggling to take command of her emotions. "I-I—lost my baby. A boy. Stillborn. That's why I was in the hospital." Brigit choked back a sob.

Kelley laid her hand on Brigit's arm. "I'm sorry—that was so insensitive of me. We've only lived here a couple of weeks. A neighbor told us you'd been in the hospital—neighborhood gossip, you know—but they didn't mention why."

"Don't worry about it. You couldn't have known." Brigit smoothed her jeans with shaking hands. "It's been a few weeks, but it hurts just as bad today as it did when he died. He was a perfect little boy in every way. Full-term. It shouldn't have happened, but it did. We don't know why. We may never know."

She needed to go back home...to the safety of the only place where she wouldn't be questioned... or asked to explain the unexplainable. Brigit rose from the folding chair and stretched. "Well, I'd better be going back home. It's my first day out of bed and I don't want to overdo it."

"You've been cooped up in your apartment for far too long. You'll be surprised how a change of scenery will invigorate you. Before you know it, you'll feel like going back to work and starting a new chapter in your life." Kelley cradled Karen in the crook of her arm, while pushing out of her chair with the other. "You'll see. Every day will get easier and one day, when you least expect it—"

"I don't mean to be rude, but that's all I hear from Will and my parents. I just don't think anyone understands." Brigit flinched at the pain in Kelley's eyes. She had hurt her feelings when all Kelley was trying to do was offer encouragement. "I'm sorry. I shouldn't have said that."

"It's okay. I probably came on a little too strong. It takes time for healing. Everyone has to go through the healing process in their own time…and their own way." Kelley laid the toddler into her playpen, covering her with a soft pink blanket.

Brigit sighed. She was amazed by her new friend's gracious reply. "Thanks for letting me talk. It helped just getting all that out. I'm just sorry I got so emotional. I only intended to return your dish and go for a walk around the block. I never meant to dump my problems on you and keep you from whatever you had planned."

"With this brood? I never plan anything. I was glad to meet you and have some adult company." Kelley hesitated and then gave Brigit a quick hug.

Brigit's eyes widened. "I just felt someone kick me!" Her mouth dropped open. "You're pregnant?"

Kelley blushed. "I'm almost five months, but being so tall, I guess I conceal it well. I didn't want to mention it, so you wouldn't…well, you know—"

"In spite of my terrible reaction a few minutes ago, I don't want you to deliberately try to spare my feelings. I know life goes on. It's just taking me a little longer than most people, I guess." She returned Kelley's warm hug.

"Okay. It is a deal. Come over anytime."

Her cropped red hair and green eyes reminded Brigit of her sister-in-law, Angie. She should call her. Thank her for the flower arrangement. See if the move had been a good one…how life was without Rick…

"Thanks. I've missed not having anyone to talk to. I mean a *girl-friend* to talk to. I find it hard to open up to Will. I know I've failed him and I guess I let that get in the way of sharing what's in my heart." She swiped at an escaping tear.

Kelley thrust a tissue into Brigit's hand. "I'm sure he doesn't blame you. That's something you're going to have to get out of your head. What happened wasn't your fault. I can say that with authority because I had two miscarriages before we had Kary. So, I know how you feel. But, I also know that God has blessed us with four beautiful children— and now this little one on the way." She placed the palms of her hands on her abdomen and smiled.

Brigit's heart skipped a beat. "So, you're a—a—"

"Christian. Don't be afraid to say it. It's a word I'm proud of. I like identifying my life with Christ." Kelley's smile remained unchanged.

Brigit shook her head. Why did this subject seem to keep coming up at every turn? "So you're *religious?* I never saw that coming. We had such a nice, normal, friendly visit." *And I thought I had made a new friend…*

Kelley chuckled. "Why shouldn't we? Christians aren't freaks. We're no different than anyone else."

"Except for what you believe and the things you do." Brigit took a step backward and onto the sidewalk, drawing what her literature professor would call a *line in the sand.*

Kelley's eyes widened and she raised her eyebrows. "The things we *do?*"

"Church on Sunday mornings, quoting the Bible in every situation—"

"Is that really so strange?"

Brigit swallowed hard and shrugged her shoulders. "Well, like I said, I'd better be getting on home. I'm kind of tired." She started across the narrow street separating the neighborhood of houses from the apartment complex.

Kelley called after her. "Brigit, I hope this won't change things between us. You need a friend right now, and I believe it's no accident that we moved into your neighborhood. I'm here for you...and I'll be praying for you."

She turned around and took a step back toward Kelley. "I'll think about it. I really do like you. And, it's not like I haven't had Christian friends before. We just agreed not to discuss religious beliefs and, for the most part, things worked out just fine. But Will's a lot less tolerant than I am, and I'm not sure he'd approve of us being friends."

"I like you, too. Just know the door is open. That's all."

Back inside the apartment, Brigit glanced into the small living room. Clothes and shoes were scattered all over. Kelley had been right. Will had been hurting, too.

She shook her head and turned back toward the kitchen. While she'd been grieving alone, she'd left Will to deal with his own disappointment and sadness by himself. He had been worrying about *her* while she'd been so self-absorbed that she hadn't even thought about *him*. Was she really so self-centered and callous?

Before she realized what she was doing, she added more hot water in the kitchen sink. She slid a dishcloth across the table and counter. As she washed and towel-dried the dishes, she thought about her time spent with Kelley. Except for the end of their conversation, she admitted that she liked being with her. It would be wonderful to have a new friend.

With Mary Ellen and Sue away, she was exhilarated by the prospect of having someone to talk with. The counselor was helpful, but she had set boundaries from the start. They were to have a strictly professional relationship. There would be no between-visit phone calls. No meeting for lunch. The more Brigit thought about it, maybe if she set some ground rules, like Kelley not mentioning God, they would be able to form a solid friendship. Maybe.

But was that really what she wanted? Wasn't it true that her thoughts kept going back to her conversation with the chaplain? Maybe she'd make an appointment with him sometime next week...No, she needed to get that out of her head. Will would be furious if he ever found out.

And the New Testament? She should find a better hiding place. If he came across it, what would she say? Could she tell him about the longing in her heart...the void the chaplain said only Jesus could fill?

She turned off the kitchen light and headed into the living room. She spent the next few minutes sorting laundry into piles and straightening up the pillows and magazines.

A smile tugged at her lips. The apartment looked like a home, again. Had all of this newfound energy come just from a change of scenery?

CHAPTER 9

HE WASN'T SURE WHY, BUT Will had been compelled to drive by his mother's house on the way home from work. He parked across the street, half-hidden behind a neighbor's overgrown oleander bushes, thinking of happier times. He experienced an odd tug-of-war: carefree childhood versus the expectations of adulthood.

He reached for the door handle, struggling between his desire to walk up to the house and back into his old life, and doing the responsible thing by returning to the apartment. He was overwhelmed by the full weight of his decisions during the past year. Decisions that took him to the small apartment across town and evenings spent alone. Life had been so simple last spring...

He was resolved to get his relationship with Brigit back on track. He was in this for the long haul. He adored her. He wouldn't let God's judgment drive them apart. He may have taken their son, but Will wouldn't allow him to take Brigit, too. He'd fight for her to the bitter end. Forming a fist with his right hand, he sucked in a breath between clenched teeth.

It really hadn't been so long ago that he had invited Brigit to dinner at the house for the first time. He had endured the meal, all the while fantasizing about driving her back to her dorm and taking her into his arms for a few minutes before returning home.

While helping his mother with the dishes, she had admonished him to "slow things down a bit." Even though any concerned parent would have voiced similar concerns when sensing a relationship was moving too quickly, his sudden anger caused him to take a defensive posture. He had yelled words he later wished he could forget, and then stormed out of the house.

It was more than a week before he finally sat down with her to talk it out. By then it was too late to follow her advice. Brigit was pregnant.

He took in a deep breath. He wouldn't let it end like this. He loved her too much. He forced himself to drive back to their dark, silent apartment. He put his key into the lock at exactly six o'clock, just as he'd done for the past month. The peeling sticker on the door read *Apartment Two*, but it felt more like an apartment for one. How long would this go on? He rested his forehead against the door and closed his eyes.

Brigit was always in the next room, but she might as well not be there at all. This kind of life wasn't good for either of them. He longed for her touch. He yearned for her to return to him…to sit across from him at dinner…to hold him as they fell asleep. Instead, he spent long hours alone at the kitchen table, filling out job applications or just staring into space.

He liked his current job, but concentrating on getting a position in management gave him something positive to do, and kept his mind on the future—moving ahead, rather than wallowing in his current stagnated existence.

He wanted to share the letter of interest he'd received in today's mail with Brigit. He had all but forgotten about sending the application, in the wake of all that had happened, but here it was, proof in his hands that persistence pays off.

Two days from now he would be given the chance to present himself before the hiring board at *Tempe Daily News.* The job would be quite a step up from his current position at the *Arizona Republic and Gazette*, as well as a sizeable increase in salary. It would be *lower* management, but still, it was management.

This was one of those times he could have used his father's insight and wisdom. But Dad wasn't here, so he'd just have to figure it out on his own. He squeezed his eyes shut and let out a deep sigh.

He pushed the door open and stepped into the small hallway. He walked toward the bedroom, expecting to see the door shut. He shook his head in disbelief. The bed was made and the air smelled like Pine Sol.

Walking in the opposite direction, he entered the living room. His jaw dropped. Instead of the ever-growing mess he was accustomed to, it was free from the clutter of newspapers and clothing.

When Brigit appeared in the doorway of the kitchen dressed in jeans and a sweatshirt, he stopped cold. *What had made the change?* He placed his briefcase on the coffee table and took one step, then another.

Brigit's smile started at the corners of her mouth and rose upward until it reached her eyes and exploded with light and magic. No one had a smile that even came close to hers.

After a moment's hesitation, she rushed to him, planting a kiss on his mouth, ever so soft and slow. "I'm glad you're home." She motioned for him to sit at the table and then turned to open the oven door. "Dinner's almost ready."

His head spun. *Had she rounded a corner? Come out the other end of that long dark tunnel that held her captive for so long?*

There was so much to say—to share—but the words just wouldn't come. Tears welled up in his eyes. He watched as the gift of a love that had become a distant memory slowly reappeared... and with it, the promise of a future filled with happier times.

He knew at this precise moment, with Brigit in their first apartment, was where he wanted to be, after all. He slipped his hand into his pocket and ran his fingers over the smooth circle of gold and the small diamond held in place by double prongs. It had served Grandma well for 50 years. Now, cleaned and polished, it would grace another hand, symbolizing his love for the wife he would cherish for the rest of his life.

———◆———

Two days later, Will whistled as he bounded down the steps of the newspaper building two at a time. He had snagged the job he wanted, but his sights were already set on upper level management. That's where the money was, the respect, and the life he wanted for Brigit and their future family. He smiled. Things were looking up.

He drove in the direction of the real estate office in downtown Phoenix. Brigit thought she was meeting him there to look at home listings. However, he had a little surprise for her. He rubbed his sweaty palms on his pants and took in a deep breath. He really did intend to look at listings—just not today.

He pulled the Mustang into a space near the front of the building, parking beside Brigit's powder blue Volkswagen. The car was already twelve years old when they'd bought it, but so far it proved to be dependable. Brigit looked radiant, waiting for him near the entrance, wearing a corduroy blazer and knitted scarf.

She met him with a soft kiss and a long hug. "Congratulations! I'm glad you called me. I couldn't have waited any longer to hear your news." She linked arms with him as they walked into the lobby.

He smiled at his soul mate. "It's definitely going to be more money than we're used to—and we'll still need to rent for a while—but now we can start saving to buy a home of our own." He held the heavy glass door open for her. "How was your session with the counselor?"

"It was good. I think it's helping. I'm grateful to Mom and Dad for paying for it." She gave his hand a squeeze. "There are a lot of feelings to sort through, but most of all I'm learning the importance of forgiving myself. Dr. Bentley says it's the only way I'm going to be able to move forward. I think she's right about that."

They walked across the expansive lobby to the bank of elevators. They waited for the next one, the display showing it was nine floors away.

He turned, raising his eyebrows. "Next week I go with you, right?"

"Yes. We'll have counseling together every week for four weeks and then we'll be on our own for six months. Of course, if we need to, we can make an appointment before then."

They stepped into the empty elevator when it arrived and Will pushed a glowing button. Once the door closed, he placed his hands on her shoulders and turned her toward him. He tipped her chin upward and pulled her close, feeling her warmth as they kissed.

Pulling back, Brigit glanced at the elevator control panel. "Oh, no! The elevator didn't stop at our floor. Now, we're here on the rooftop."

The door opened and he stepped out, offering her his hand. A sly smile played on his lips. "We may as well see the view before we go back down, don't you think?"

———◆———

Brigit cocked her head and squinted her eyes. Will was acting so—different. "What's going on?"

"You'll see." Will placed her arm in the crook of his and led her onto the terrace dotted with large pots of greenery, some with blooming succulents.

The roof was almost entirely glass cut into triangular shapes. Light bounced off the surfaces, casting rainbows in every direction.

She left his side, then opened her arms wide and twirled around taking in the majestic mountains on the skyline encircling the tall building. Oranges and purples tinged a fiery sunset. "Will, this is amazing! It couldn't be more beautiful, don't you think?" She paused. "Will?" She pivoted, her breath catching when she saw him.

He smiled from ear-to-ear, a bouquet of yellow daisies in his hands. He bent down on one knee. "Brig, you deserve a long speech, music, and violins. You deserve so much more than I will ever be able to give you." His voice started to break up and his chin quivered.

Her eyes widened and she pressed her hands against her cheeks. "Oh, my goodness. Are you doing what I think you're doing?"

He paused and nodded. "I hope you know I love you. I want nothing more than to be your husband. I hope you'll say you want to be my wife."

She had dreamed of this day for so long. She drew in a quick breath. "Oh, Will! All of this couldn't be more perfect. I love you with all my heart. Yes! Yes! I'll marry you!"

He jumped to his feet, took her into his arms, and bent her backward, giving her a "Sailor/Nurse Kiss" made famous at the close of World War II—one she would never forget. They sat on a cozy bench and snuggled as the sun dipped low in the sky and dusk settled over the mountains in the distance.

His voice was barely above a whisper. "May I put a ring on your finger?"

She gasped, a smile mingling with the tears in her eyes. "You have a ring? How did you...I mean—"

"It was the wedding set that Grandpa Hayes gave to Grandma more than 50 years ago. He got her a larger diamond years later, but she told me she always preferred this simple setting. I hope you'll feel the same." He slipped the golden circle out of his pocket and onto her finger.

When she held it out in front of her, a shooting star illuminated the sky just long enough for her to catch a glimpse of the small diamond glistening on her hand. She marveled at the perfection of the moment.

His voice was soft and low. "I planned that, you know."

"I'm sure of it."

———◆———

Two weeks later, on the Saturday morning after New Year's, Brigit smoothed the skirt of her soft blue dress with nervous hands. She loved the eyelet trim on the neck and sleeves; its darker shade of blue a perfect complement to her eyes. Though not expensive, it was one of the most beautiful dresses she had ever seen.

She'd bought it almost a year earlier, to wear to a friend's wedding. Two days before the event she contracted a virus and was unable to attend. The dress hung in her closet for months, waiting for just the right occasion.

She peered into the mirror. Did she look like a bride? Maybe she should wear just a touch of blush and lipstick… She drew one side of her hair back with her grandmother's tortoise shell comb, reasoning that even a hat and a short veil would have looked out of place.

It was Will who had suggested they marry in front of the Justice of the Peace by the bench where they had met on the ASU campus. Only a handful of people had been invited: Derf; Grace, a co-worker of Brigit's; and Will's mother, Gretchen. Brigit's parents had been invited, too, but since they had just flown to Arizona a month before, after the loss of the baby, they couldn't afford the cost of plane tickets a second time. Brigit was disappointed, but she understood.

She had missed sleeping with Will last night. He'd stayed at Derf's so that she could have enough space to get ready by herself and have time to spend with Grace. Girl talk was all it ended up being. She hadn't wanted to talk about the loss of the baby or any of that sadness. She was dealing with all that in her counseling sessions. She would never forget her baby, but she felt stronger now, ready to move on.

She'd had her postpartum check up the day before and was given a clean bill of health. They had two more weeks of counseling left. She no longer worried about trying to hurt herself again. Everything was back to normal...or at least as normal as it could be.

They'd be married when a new baby was conceived. Will thought that would make all the difference. It was out of character for him to care what God thought, but if doing things God's way would insure a healthy baby, like his mother seemed to imply, he said he was willing to do everything by the book. No sense taking chances.

She stared at the cloudless sky through the bedroom window. She wasn't sure she still shared Will's opinion of God. She'd been reading the New Testament, little by little, when he was at work. The picture she was forming in her mind was that of a loving God—one who cared about each person, forgiving their shortcomings rather than punishing them.

She bowed her head. *God, I don't know you, but the chaplain says you know me. If that's true, can I ask you a favor? Will you bless our marriage and help us to find our way?* As she finished praying, she felt an unfamiliar sense of peace.

Today she'd start married life with a clean slate. She'd marry the boy of her dreams who had grown into the man she'd always wanted to marry. They'd plan their lives and chart their course. Life would be smooth sailing from now on.

Will had been adamant about not inviting Gretchen to the wedding. He wanted to call her *afterward* and tell her the big news—when it would be too late for her to do anything about it. Brigit's future mother-in-law hadn't said as much, but Will was sure she felt the baby's death happened as a result of God's judgment on the "out of wedlock" pregnancy—and the fact that they had been living together for the last six months.

Once Brigit had pointed out to him that the wedding would be sure to change Gretchen's feelings about any future pregnancies, he had finally relented and extended the invitation. Maybe they would be able to "mend their fences" as her grandpa Dawson used to say and get off to a new start.

Her stomach rumbled as she practiced a few smiles in the mirror. Grace had eaten a bowl of cereal, but Brigit had decided to wait until after the ceremony to eat. She and Will planned to take their friends to an early lunch at The Chuckbox after the ceremony. It was all they could afford, but she had been honest when she told Will that, money or not, it was the perfect place for them to celebrate.

A knock at the front door broke into her thoughts. Grace was still in the shower. She'd have to answer it herself and take the chance it wasn't Will. After all, it was bad luck for the groom to see the bride before the wedding. She rushed to the door and flung it open.

Her neighbor stood on her doorstep, smiling like a Cheshire cat.

"Kelley!"

"Two little lost birdies told me you were getting married this morning." Her eyes glistened as she smiled.

"Oh, I...I..." She frowned into the morning sun. "What do you mean, '*two* little *lost* birdies'?"

"Us!" Brigit's parents appeared from around the corner. "We ended up on Kelley's doorstep by mistake and she was nice enough to bring us on over."

Her heart skipped a beat when she heard their voices. "I didn't think you could come. Now that you're here, everything is perfect!" Everyone she loved—and who loved her—would be with them on their wedding day.

"Listen, about not seeing you at the hospital. That was so rude of me. You'd come such a long way and—" Brigit blurted out her long overdue apology.

"Now, now. Let's not talk about that today. We understood what you were going through. We probably expected too much. Let's leave it at that." Her father gave her hand a squeeze and led her back into the apartment.

Her mother followed, closing the door behind her. "We're glad to be here, honey. We wouldn't have missed this day for the world. Now, don't cry. You have to keep it together so you don't ruin your makeup, you hear? Nobody wants to see a bride with a blotchy face and raccoon eyes!"

"Oh, no! Kelley's out there. I'll be back in a minute." Brigit opened the door, calling to her neighbor as she walked back across the street. "Kelley, wait!"

Kelley turned and faced Brigit with a big smile. "Don't worry about me. I understand. Just go be with your parents. I'll talk to you later." Kelley shooed her back inside.

"No. Listen. I want to explain." Brigit hurried forward to join her on the sidewalk. "I didn't tell you about the wedding because you assumed we were already married, and I was too embarrassed to correct you. I-I didn't want you to judge me. I'm sorry." She lowered her head, focusing on the web of cracks in the pavement.

"It's okay. Really. But, Brigit there is only one judge—and I'm not Him." She gave Brigit a tight hug. "Congratulations."

Brigit smiled, returning the embrace. "Thank you. And, um, Kelley, I've missed you. Let's get together in a few days, okay? Before I go back to work?"

"Sure. I'd like that." She gave Brigit a quick wave, as she walked across her yard, gathering up stray toys as she went.

———————

An hour later, under a picture-perfect sky, Brigit's hand trembled as Will nervously slipped the wedding band next to her engagement ring. She barely heard the words of the ceremony. All she could think about was how handsome he looked in his long-sleeved blue shirt—the same shade as her dress—and striped tie. He was every bit the person she thought him to be: kind, caring, selfless. She truly was happy on this, her wedding day. The dark cloud hanging over them the last few months had lifted. Perhaps a rainbow was just around the corner...

She turned her attention back to Will, his crystal blue eyes twinkling in the midmorning light. He rubbed his thumb over the top of her hand and winked at her the way he had so many times before.

She savored the traditional kiss, long and gentle. It brought a sense of rightness to her wedding day. She smiled at the small group of onlookers as she raised the simple bouquet of daisies overhead. She was Mrs. Will Hayes!

———————

Will closed his eyes, inhaling the crisp morning breeze. Everything was perfect. Was it his imagination, or was the air more fragrant...the sky bluer?

Sixteen days ago, Brigit had come back to him. And, in those days, they had talked—really talked—to one another about everything that had happened since the first day they met. And, through the sharing of their hopes, their dreams—their very souls—they had grown closer than ever before. What a turn their lives had taken!

As soon as the ceremony was over, his mother rushed forward and placed an angel pin onto the shoulder of Brigit's dress. "I'm so happy for you both, dears." She gave Will a long hug before she stepped back and allowed Brigit's parents to congratulate them, too.

Brigit had been right in her assessment that lunch at The Chuckbox was the perfect place to culminate their wedding day. Derf had gone all out, decorating the place with yellow and blue streamers and white balloons. He even made special burgers, with baked potatoes as substitutes for the usual French fries, and a delicious cranberry punch.

His mother had contributed a small cake to the festivities, covered with yellow daisies and topped with traditional bride and groom figurines. He thought it looked out of place on the red-and-white checked tablecloth, next to the platter of burgers, but Brigit seemed pleased with it. The cover of a *Bride* magazine displayed in the grocery store checkout line said, "Happy Bride, Happy Wife." That summed it up.

Will mouthed *I love you* across the room to Brigit as he talked about the upcoming Super Bowl with her father. His mind wasn't on the game, though. It was on the cherub his mother had placed on her shoulder. He appreciated the *appearance* of thoughtfulness behind her gift, but couldn't help wondering about its *real* significance.

CHAPTER 10

LEGS DANGLING OVER THE SIDE of the bed, Brigit raised her arms and stretched. She turned back to look at Will in the early morning light. He was still sleeping soundly. He was her husband—devoted, handsome, and patient beyond her understanding.

Last night, their wedding night, had been spent in the airport terminal chatting with her parents as they waited for their flight back to Indiana. It had been such a nice conversation, a time of bonding with their new son-in-law.

At the time, she hadn't given a thought to the fact that perhaps Will was looking forward to their first night of married life alone. By the time they checked into their room at the Holiday Inn—a gift from her parents—it was two o'clock in the morning. They were both so tired they had fallen asleep on the king-size bed wearing their wedding clothes.

She crept into the bathroom, closed the door, and turned on the water in the shower. While waiting for it to warm, she unzipped her wedding dress and gently placed it on a hanger. Although inexpensive—and now beyond wrinkled and in dire need of dry-cleaning—she would treasure it forever.

She slid back the green and gold shower curtain and stepped inside, pulling it closed and enjoying the luxurious warmth of the pulsating water. She ran the smooth bar of soap over her stomach, then her arms, before pouring the shampoo onto her head and working up a rich lather.

Yesterday was a blur—the vows, the kiss, tossing her bouquet, and Will's crystal blue eyes. She vowed to save each memory in her heart through the coming years... reliving them over and over again...the happiest of days. Lost as she was in her thoughts, she almost didn't hear the soft knock on the door.

"Brig?"

"Yes?" She turned off the water, pulled back the curtain, and reached for a towel. She ran its softness over her face and hair. She opened her eyes and smiled, her lips slightly parted. "You're awake."

Will's face was inches away. He took the towel from her hands and gently dried her body, then her hair, all the while kissing her neck and shoulders. Then, he picked her up and carried her back to bed.

———————

It was half past eleven when Will woke. He nuzzled Brigit awake. "We need to get dressed and take advantage of the continental breakfast before they close it down at noon."

"Um, I'm starved." She gave him a quick kiss, pulled jeans and a sweater out of her overnight bag, and slipped them on. She brushed back her hair and caught it into her grandmother's turquoise shell clip, and was ready to go before Will even started getting ready.

"Hey, what have you been doing? Just standing there?" Brigit's eyes gleamed.

"Oh, just admiring my beautiful wife," Will answered.

"It's 11:30. Hurry up. I'm looking forward to a free meal."

Will rummaged around in his bag for his jeans. He pulled his Arizona State sweatshirt over his head and stumbled toward the bathroom. He thought back to yesterday's events. He didn't remember every detail, but he did recall vividly the moment he slipped the wedding band on Brigit's finger. He and Brigit were actually married!

There wasn't much left on the buffet table by the time he and Brigit arrived—just a few muffins, sausage, cold eggs, and orange juice—but to Will, it tasted delicious. He continued to sneak peaks at his new wife between bites. Other than the reception, this was their first meal together as a married couple. He reached for her hand, brought it to his lips, and sealed his love for her with a hint of marmalade.

After they ate, there was just enough time to take a quick swim in the pool, pack their few things, and check out by 2 p.m. With their suitcase still in the trunk of the Mustang, they stopped by the market on their way back to their apartment. Tomorrow was the first day on his new job. He'd take his lunch. They couldn't afford for him to spend money on eating at restaurants.

He splurged late in the afternoon by taking Brigit to a movie, complete with popcorn and sodas. It wasn't the fanciest of honeymoons, but the movie was a romantic comedy and his new bride seemed to enjoy every minute. He kissed her forehead and she slipped her hand into his, laying her head on his shoulder.

They walked back home, dancing around light poles—their own version of *Singing in the Rain*—not caring if anyone was watching or what they might think. The woes of the past nine months were behind them, and Will was ready for the challenges ahead in the newspaper office and in his role as a husband. With Brigit by his side, he could handle most anything.

———

Brigit waved Will off to work from the living room window the next morning, slipped on her tennis shoes, grabbed a light jacket, and locked the front door. Today would be her last chance for a brisk walk because tomorrow she'd return to the hospital full time. Just twenty-four hours from now, and life would be back to how it was before... before... No, she wouldn't think negative thoughts. And self-blame served no purpose.

She would choose life, rich and full. She would move forward with Will, knowing that someday she would see her baby again—alive and well, a vibrant little boy. She had to believe that. The very thought— the hope—that they'd someday be reunited would give her reason to face the future.

As hard as it was to admit to herself, to her therapist, and finally to Will, they hadn't been ready to be parents. Not then. But, they had learned a lot over these last months—a lot about caring for babies, and a lot about each other. They would use this time, while it was just the two of them, to grow together and build a solid marriage that would be the basis of a nurturing family life for their future children.

Forty minutes later, she stopped to catch her breath. She looked up at the street sign. Maple Street. Her eyes drifted over to the corner house with its low fence, manicured shrubs and flowering succulents. Gretchen's house.

Her mother-in-law's car was in the driveway. Should she ring the bell? Would she welcome a visit from her new daughter-in-law? Now that her own mother had gone back to Indiana, she found herself long-ing for the companionship of a mother figure. Maybe she'd convince Will that they should drop by to see Gretchen sometime over the week-end. That might be better.

She headed back down the street, amazed that she'd walked a full three miles, and aware that she needed to hurry to get the laundry done at the Laundromat before Will got home from work. What a luxury it would be to someday have a washer and dryer of their very own.

"Brigit. What a delightful surprise!"

She made an about-face.

Gretchen had a watering can in one hand and a spade in the other. Her bangs, wet with perspiration, hung in a cluster of curls. Her smile emphasized her dimples...just like Will's.

Brigit gulped. Should she let Gretchen know this was just a chance meeting or let her think it had been planned? "Hi! I thought about ringing the bell, but then I noticed what time it was and wasn't sure I'd have enough time to visit and still get the laundry done before Will gets home."

"Oh, dear, a visit would be lovely. How about we have some coffee and talk?" Gretchen raised her eyebrows and smiled. "If I drive you back home, you'll be right on schedule to get your chores done." She set down her gardening tools and took hold of Brigit's elbow, guiding her toward the door.

Brigit hesitated, then bit her lip, and grinned. "Sure. Why not? I go back to work tomorrow. Who knows when we'll have a chance to do this, again."

She followed Gretchen in the side door off the carport and into the spacious kitchen. She drank in the smell of cinnamon and nutmeg. This house always smelled so good...felt so peaceful.

"Are you sure I'm not keeping you from your plans?"

Gretchen poured coffee into two ceramic mugs, placed a few blueberry scones on a delicate glass plate, and brought them to the table. "Not at all. In fact, I chided myself for making a full pot of coffee this morning. I usually only make enough for me, but today, for some reason, I made more. I guess the Lord was preparing me for a special visitor."

Brigit took a bite of a delicious scone and closed her eyes. Did God really care about the little things in life enough to nudge someone to make an extra cup or two of coffee?

———————

Brigit sat down across from Will. If she didn't tell him she spent time with Gretchen, he wouldn't understand how she had been home a full ten hours and still had two baskets of dirty laundry in the trunk of the car. "I saw your mom, today."

He cocked his head and raised his eyebrows. "Oh? How did that happen?"

"I didn't mean to go over there, but I took a walk this morning and just somehow ended up on Maple Street. Gretchen was gardening and—"

"She invited you in for coffee. Just like that." His face reddened.

"Yeah. How did you know?"

"Because that's her favorite way of worming her way into people's lives, their confidences, and gaining their trust. Oh, believe me, it's not just her way of being friendly. She always has an ulterior motive." He scowled.

"And just what so-called ulterior motive would she possibly have in this case?" After all, Gretchen hadn't even known Brigit was going to pop by for a visit.

Will rolled his eyes. "Divide and conquer."

"Excuse me?"

"You know. She gets you over there. Offers you a cup of coffee and a muffin or scone—which are fabulous, I admit—then she pretends to listen to all of your trivial talk about our future plans. All the while she's getting this little friendship off the ground without me around to run interference and keep her nose out of our business. Am I right?"

His eyes bore into hers as he paused, waiting for her confirmation of events just as he surmised they had happened.

Brigit cleared her throat and took a long sip of water. She had been excited to share those things. Gretchen hadn't coerced her into talking. The entire visit was pleasant...comfortable... Now Will was making her feel as though she'd been used as a pawn in a game between the two of them. "I guess you could say that—"

"Bingo." Will leaned back in his chair, smiling like a kid in a candy store.

"You know, sometimes the way you talk, I get the impression that you've got some sort of vendetta against your mother." Brigit pushed away from the table to get a box of crackers from the cupboard. She'd give anything for the luxury of being able to walk across town and visit *her* mother. Why was he so cold to Gretchen?

"Oh, of course I love her. It's just that I *know* her...how she operates. And you just proved my point." He took his bowl to the stovetop and ladled himself a second helping of chili. "Take my advice and steer clear of her. If you don't, you'll end up getting sucked into something you're not prepared to handle."

"What do you mean?"

"It's obvious, isn't it? She's going to try to convert you to Christianity. She'll invite you to church, or maybe a Bible Study group. Who knows? Maybe she'll get you a Bible with your name engraved on it for Christmas. Just remember, I told you so."

Brigit looked down at her still-untouched dinner. She was no longer hungry. What if he was right and she'd already gone too far...opened up too much?

"And, since we're on the subject, I'm going to throw my two cents in about your friend across the street, too. She's cut from the same cloth as my mother."

Brigit jumped to her feet. "Will, I don't tell you who you can and can't be friends with!"

"I know. I know. But, I'm just warning you. Believe me, you'll thank me later."

———

"Derf! Buddy, it's good to see you." Will pushed his grocery cart aside and gave his best friend a pat on the back, followed by their "secret" handshake. They had made it up in junior high and it remained their favorite greeting, even as adults. They extended right hands, placing palms together and sliding them in one direction and then the other. They finished by bumping knuckles, and then shoulders.

"What's it been? Almost two weeks?"

"Yeah. We used to talk every day. But it takes time to settle into married life and all."

"I understand. Are you all by yourself?" Derf's eyes scanned the produce section.

"No. Brigit's on the other side of the store searching for some coupon items. I couldn't find them, so she's now doing my job and I'm in charge of the rest of the shopping." Will pulled a handwritten list from his shirt pocket and held it up. "She should be wandering back this way any minute."

"So, how's married life treating you two? Getting along okay?"

"We're doing fine, I guess. We've got our home and work routines pretty much set. Brigit's back full time at the hospital and I've been working long hours. We're both beat when we roll in, but things will improve."

"Am I wrong, or do I catch just a hint of something in your voice? Like maybe things aren't quite as perfect as you thought they'd be?"

"Oh, it's just that Mom and Brigit are becoming friends—"

Derf interrupted. "With all the stories of mother-in-law problems, I'd think you'd find it refreshing to know they actually like each other."

"I know. You'd think so, but the thing is that I know my mother. She figures if she can't get anywhere with me on the 'God thing', she'll try to get at me through the back door—that door being Brigit."

Derf hesitated, and then looked Will in the eyes. "Maybe you should try to look at it from a different perspective."

"What do you mean?"

"Maybe she's just concerned for your wife's spiritual life. Couldn't it be that she's not using any devious tactics where *you* are concerned? Maybe she's just treating Brigit as a person in her own right—her and her alone. Couldn't it be that it's Brigit's well-being Gretchen is thinking of and it has nothing to do with you?"

Will could feel his face turn crimson. "You're wrong about that. Who is Mom to think she knows what is best for Brigit? I'm her husband. I love her. I want only the best for her. There's no way I'd intentionally make a life for us that would end up hurting her or making her unhappy."

Derf put his hand on Will's shoulder. "I know you wouldn't do that on purpose, but I believe if you don't let Brigit make her own decisions about God and his rightful place in her life, she *will* end up hurt and unhappy."

"You're beginning to sound just like my—"

"Brigit!" Derf's face brightened when she came around the corner.

"Hi, Derf. Good to see you." Brigit gave him a hug and walked back to stand at Will's side.

"You look great. Guess married life is treating you well." He smiled and raised his eyebrows.

"Couldn't be happier." Brigit gave Will's hand a squeeze.

He drooped his arm around Brigit's shoulders and gave her a kiss on the top of her head. "Any luck? I see you still have a hand full of coupons."

"I couldn't find them, either. Guess we're stuck with buying from the 'Smart Buys' in this flyer." She handed Will the paper and tapped her finger on the ground beef special. "I'll be at the meat counter. You two take your time visiting." Brigit headed off toward the back of the store, then turned and called out, "Hey, Derf, don't be a stranger."

Will studied Derf's face before he spoke. "She's right, you know. You're welcome to drop by any time. But, I don't want you filling Brigit's head with a lot of nonsense. When we first met, she and I talked about this issue. We both felt—and still feel—the same way about God. We don't need you, Mom, and Kelley, causing arguments between us."

"But, Will—"

"I mean it, Derf. Don't put me in a position where I have to choose between you and Brigit. You know I'll choose her every time."

———◆———

As she walked toward the meat counter, Brigit heard Kelley's voice. She turned sideways to see her friend pushing a cart overflowing with kids. She hadn't seen her since the morning of the wedding.

Brigit swallowed hard. She'd promised she would visit, but had neglected to get in touch. She felt guilty and probably should apologize, but instead she plastered a smile on her face. "Kelley!"

She tilted her chin in Brigit's direction. "It's good to see you, Brigit. Just wiping a few runny noses. I dropped off their prescriptions at the pharmacy and thought I might have time to run in here for a few things before they're ready for pick-up."

Brigit ran her hand over the soft golden curls on the youngest child's head. "Well, I can see you have your hands full. I'll see you at home sometime." She guided her cart closer to the meat counter and took a number from the dispenser.

Kelley followed her. "You know, we really should set a date and time to have coffee. If we don't, I'm afraid this baby will be here before we have a chance to get together. And then, you know, I'll be busy with all that. Then there's always the possibility of a military transfer for Jim—"

Brigit frowned. "Transfer...military...I had no idea."

"Yeah, didn't you notice the sign on the corner, across from the entrance to our neighborhood? It says 'Military Housing.' I thought you knew." She pulled a handful of tissues from her purse and wiped yet another runny nose.

"I don't usually come in that way. I probably saw it at one time or another, but I guess it just didn't register for some reason."

"Yeah. It seems like every time I start making friends, we get transferred."

"I'll miss you."

"I'll miss you, too." Kelley gave her an unexpected hug. "But, a transfer could be months away, so let's not get teary eyed just yet."

"Well, I'm back at work at the hospital now, and my schedule is kind of crazy, but I have Thursday and Friday off next week."

"How about next Thursday?"

"Sure. I'll pop over about 2:00."

"Sounds great."

Brigit's number was called and she waved good-bye. She felt like she'd been kicked in the stomach. True, she hadn't gotten in touch with Kelley as she had promised, so why the stab of loss at hearing the friendship she *could* have developed with her might never be?

Who knows? Maybe her husband wouldn't get transferred, after all. Or, maybe it would be like she thought at first...an awkward friendship between herself and a believer. It might have never worked out. Maybe her moving would be for the best, after all.

She smiled when she thought of Kelley and that cart full of children. She showed such patience with her cranky kids, remaining calm even when they grabbed at each other or whined for candy. Brigit could almost imagine a halo around her head. One day, she'd love to be that kind of mom.

———◆———

Will came through the door with a smile on his face and more energy at the end of the day than he had experienced in the last three months. The smell of pot roast was a welcome surprise. He tiptoed into the kitchen, grabbing Brigit from behind.

She gasped. "Will! You know I don't like it when you sneak up on me." Her stern look melted into a smile. She turned toward him, put her arms around his neck and planted a kiss on his lips.

"You'll forgive me when you see what I found." He thrust a folded newspaper into her hands. A two-inch square of the copy had been circled and starred in red ink.

As Brigit read the ad, a smile formed at the corners of her mouth. "It sounds just like what we've been looking for. Have you called about it, yet?"

He snapped his fingers. "That I have, my love. We can drive out there after dinner and meet with the agent, if it's okay with you." His eyebrows moved up and down as he did his favorite imitation of Groucho Marx. He grabbed her by the hands and twirled her around the kitchen, finally stopping to let her catch her breath.

"Actually… it would be… perfect if we found a place, today, because… I have some news of my own to share." Brigit opened a cupboard door, took out a pineapple upside down cake, and placed it at the far end of the kitchen table.

"Wow! My favorite." Will nuzzled her neck, then pulled back to look her in the eyes. "It's not our anniversary or my birthday…so what gives? Did you get a raise?"

"Nope. Let's eat. I'll tell you when we have dessert." Brigit pulled the roast out of the oven.

Will cocked his head and narrowed his eyes. "Is this roast part of the surprise? I don't remember buying one on Saturday."

"No. Gretchen brought it over this afternoon. She had a dinner party last night and the roast and vegetables were left over. She thought we might like it and knew it would be a treat for me not to have to cook. It was very thoughtful of her, don't you think?" She placed the hot pad on the table and peeled the foil back from the steaming meat.

Will breathed in the aroma. His mom's pot roast was his favorite. "It was nice of her. But just remember what I said before. She's up to something. I can feel it. But, let's eat and get on the road. Dessert can wait until we get back. Right?" Will filled his plate, and then held the dish toward Brigit.

"Did I say something wrong?"

Her eyes fluttered open. "No, why?"

"Because you sometimes close your eyes when you're upset about something."

"I do?" She looked at him, batting them innocently.

"Yes, you do." Whatever it was, he wouldn't push it. After dinner, they had a house to see—and an affordable one at that.

"I hadn't noticed. Anyway, nothing's wrong." She busied herself with buttering her potato and layering her meat with gravy.

"Then why *were* your eyes closed?"

———◆———

Kelley's kids were down for their naps, her house oddly quiet. Brigit picked up two stoneware mugs filled with hot coffee, poured in cream and sugar, and stirred. She had a good view from Kelley's window of her own apartment across the street. She'd be able to see when Will's car turned the corner. By the time he parked in their reserved spot in the back, she could dash home—and he'd be none the wiser.

Her friend emerged from the bathroom and joined her at the table. "Thanks for pouring the coffee. It seems like these days if I'm not changing diapers or fixing snacks for the kids, I'm in the bathroom." She placed a blue leather Bible on the edge of the table.

Brigit took a gulp of coffee and stuffed a jelly-filled donut in her mouth. Maybe Will was right. What gave Kelley the idea that she was open to talking about God? "Kelley, what are you doing?"

"Oh, I'm just putting my Bible out to remind me to prepare for my Bible Study Group, tomorrow morning. Five of us ladies meet here at 9:00 each Friday. We're studying the book of John. You're always welcome to join us."

"I don't know if I—"

"I could loan you a Bible, if you want," Kelley interrupted, placing her hand on Brigit's. "I do wish you'd open yourself up to God. You may not know it yet, but you need Him in your life."

Brigit shook her head. "Maybe, but sometimes it seems like He's *pushing* His way into my life—ready or not."

"What do you mean?"

"Oh, you know, just all the stuff with losing our baby and all..." She let her voice trail off, hoping Kelley wouldn't insist that she talk about that dark time and voice her thoughts about how she now viewed God's involvement in her life—and Will's. She wasn't sure just how she felt, or even if she could put her feelings into words, yet.

"Okay. Just know you're welcome, when you feel ready. No pressure."

"I'm not a complete heathen, you know."

Kelley's hand, still on hers, gave her a gentle squeeze. "Oh, Brigit, I didn't mean to imply anything of the sort. It's just that I've been a Christian for a long, long time, and I still need to learn and grow in my faith."

Brigit hesitated. She's probably moving, soon. It wouldn't hurt to open up to her just a little bit. "I've been talking to my mother-in-law. She's a Christian, too. And I do have a New Testament. I read it on my lunch break at work, sometimes."

Kelley's smile seemed to erupt from a place of pure joy. She poured more coffee into their mugs and mouthed, "Yes!"

"But, just because I'm open to learning, doesn't mean I want to be singled out as a new convert or anything."

"You can ask all the questions you want. There's not anything one of us hasn't asked at one time or another. We're all here to help—and pray for—each group member."

Brigit glanced out the window and down the street. Her heart began to beat a little faster as she looked for the Mustang to round the corner. "That's another thing. I wouldn't want to pray out loud or do any of that other Christian stuff. I'd be better off sitting in a corner, just absorbing."

"If that's what you're comfortable doing, you can do just that. When you're ready to participate, you can. Until then, just observe and absorb, as you put it."

———◆———

"I've got good news. They accepted our offer on the house!" Will threw his briefcase down in the old recliner and walked over to the sofa where Brigit lay asleep, her head resting on one of the bright yellow pillows they had purchased at a summer clearance. He bent down to sit on the coffee table, watching as she breathed in and out, sighing intermittently, her eyes rolling back and forth under her lids as she dreamed. It was a shame to wake her. He worried about her lately. She seemed to be having a hard time getting used to working full time.

He looked toward the kitchen. The table was set. Two plates. Dinner was cold. He hadn't planned on working so late, but as more and more people moved to the Valley of the Sun, the newspaper's distribution grew, and the more complex his job became. They said they would hire someone to help him by the end of summer, but he had his doubts.

"Brig...Honey...How about some dinner?" He shook her shoulders.

Brigit yawned, stretched, and opened one eye. "Oh, did I fall asleep?" She sat up, cross-legged. "Whoa. Is that clock right? Eight o'clock?"

"Yeah, sorry. I had lots of work to do. I'm going to put dinner back in the pan. I can take a shower while it reheats." He walked into the kitchen and rummaged around to find the right-sized pan and lid.

When he grabbed the plates from the table, he noticed the cake Brigit had baked the day before. Hadn't she said something about a surprise? It had been almost eleven o'clock when they got back home. They both were beat by then, but still it was thoughtless of him to forget about her news. It must have been important if she had made a cake... He poked it with a fork. It was dried out and as hard as a rock. He ran his fingers through his hair and shook his head. Maybe he could wash it down later with a hot cup of coffee.

He shoved the pan into the oven and walked back into the living room. Brigit was asleep, again. Snoring this time. He'd let her sleep while he showered. Maybe she had helped his mom that afternoon, like she'd planned. They sure were seeing quite a bit of each other the past couple of weeks. Whatever they were doing seemed to be tiring Brigit out. Gardening, perhaps?

Something about their budding relationship bothered him. Was it the "God thing?" Or was it the fact that he now felt a little guilty at not making more of an effort to spend time with his mother, himself. Maybe it was time that he 'mended fences,' as Grandma would put it.

He toweled off from his shower and dressed in his drawstring pants and T-shirt. He pulled on a thick pair of tube socks and skidded down the hallway en route to the kitchen.

Brigit was sitting at the kitchen table. "Eat," she ordered and thrust a fork in his hand.

She had placed the entire cake in front of him, a large glass of milk beside it.

"What? You want me to eat dessert, first?"

Her eyes sparkled. "This time I do." She placed her elbows on the table and cradled her chin in her palms.

He frowned, studying her face. Had she been crying? He attempted to stick his fork into it, but it felt—and looked—more like a giant hockey puck, than a cake. "I'm sorry, Brig. I just don't think I'm going to be able to eat it."

Brigit jumped up from her seat, towering over him. "You have to. You have to." Tears streamed down her cheeks and onto her lips.

"Okay. Don't cry. I'll try this." Will put down the fork, picked up the cake and cracked it open against the edge of the table. "What in the world?" A slightly melted—and definitely broken—baby rattle fell onto his plate, beads scattering like confetti across the surface.

CHAPTER 11

IT WAS GETTING NEAR THE baby's due date. Will found himself daydreaming as he drove home. This new chapter in their lives had begun with Brigit's unusual "cake announcement" and seemed to have taken on an easy rhythm from that point forward.

A lot had happened in the last seven months. His improved relationship with his mother was foremost on the list. Brigit had been right to keep nudging him in the direction of an apology. Even though he didn't feel that their estrangement had been one hundred percent his fault, his heartfelt talk with his mother had gone a long way toward their reconciliation. And he had to admit, the easing of the tension between them had allowed everyone to share this special time together.

Will's raise, their purchase of the home in Apache Junction, and his joining the softball team with Derf by his side rounded out the list of positive changes. He was beginning to see how important friendships and family relationships could be...just how much he and Brigit needed love and support.

He parked the Mustang behind Brigit's VW Bug, now dubbed the "Baby Buggy." The days were starting to get shorter, as fall approached. It was only 6:00 in the evening, but it was already getting dark. He flicked the light on as he entered the kitchen, tossing his keys into the bowl in the center of the table.

The sink was full of dishes. An almost-full glass of iced tea had created a ring of moisture on the Formica countertop. The room was spacious, but still needed some remodeling. They had already painted the walls a soft brown and replaced the old refrigerator with a side-by-side, but a new dishwasher and a range and oven were still on Brigit's wish list.

"Brig, I'm back. We won the game!" He walked down the hallway, turning on the light as he entered the master bedroom. Its glow illuminated the soft blues and browns of the paint and coordinating bedspread. "Brig?" His heart skipped a beat. He had heard her right, hadn't he? They were going out to dinner at seven o'clock with Derf and his new girlfriend, Tammy. Shouldn't she be getting ready by now?

He turned and walked back through the house, stopping for a brief moment to peek into the nursery. He had painted the walls a light cream last weekend, and Brigit had placed the crib sheets and curtains, in soft yellows and browns, in the room afterward.

Will hoped for a boy, although Brigit might find it easier to have a girl at this point. It had been rough going for a while. She was doing better, but having a boy might dredge up old memories—and that might not be the best thing for her right now. There was always enough time for them to have another boy, later. After all, they both wanted a big family.

He walked back into the bedroom and turned the water on in the shower. He grabbed a towel from the stack of folded laundry and hung it on the hook at the end of the wall. Turning back toward the sink, his eyes caught Brigit's note scribbled in bright pink lipstick across the mirror: *Daddy, meet me at the hospital.*

He caught a glimpse of himself in the mirror as the wide smile that spread across his face faded. Wild-eyed, he turned off the water, and grabbed a shirt and jeans. He almost tripped as he dressed, racing down the hall toward the kitchen. He retrieved his keys and headed outside, walking around Brigit's car. He hadn't been there to drive her to the hospital. So how had she gotten there?

Once inside the Mustang, he revved the engine. Before backing out, he willed himself to slow down by taking deep calming breaths. Feelings of excitement struggled against the fearful memories of their last trip to the hospital. A shiver ran through him. He needed to be there with Brigit...

——•——

The contractions had been five minutes apart when Brigit finally broke down and made two phone calls—one to Gretchen and one to summon an ambulance. It was still a week before her due date, so they hadn't been concerned about Will going to the baseball game.

She had planned on catching up on her Bible lesson and enjoying a long afternoon nap, but instead she had been rushed to the hospital. The ambulance ride was a bit calmer compared to the last trip she had taken to Labor and Delivery...the panic on Will's face...his efforts to comfort her...

Yes, this trip had been different. She hadn't been afraid. She had felt God's presence with her as she prayed for a healthy baby, an easy birth, and that Will would get there in time for them to share His miracle together.

Her nurse and good friend, Nancy, entered the hospital room. Her hair was covered, and she had changed into surgical scrubs. Holding Brigit's hand through yet another contraction, she smiled at Gretchen. "You'll need to have a seat in the waiting room, now. I'll let you know when your grandchild is born." She pulled the bed away from the wall and pushed it toward the open door. "Let's have a baby!"

"Re-really? Can't we…wait…a little…longer?" Brigit questioned, amid panting and sucking in ragged breaths.

"Not if you don't want your baby being born out here." Nancy guided the gurney out into the hallway and headed toward the delivery room.

"Gretchen! Gretchen!" She reached out to grab her mother-in-law's hand. This was going to happen with or without Will. They had planned and looked forward to this big moment. She hoped he wouldn't miss it. *Please, God, let him make it here in time.*

Nancy's compassionate eyes met Brigit's. "I'm sorry Will's not here, but as you know, babies can't be kept waiting."

"Can Gretchen come in with me? Pl-please…?" Brigit half-spoke, half-panted her request.

"She's not Lamaze certified, Brigit. You'll be fine. I'll be with you." She hit the button on the wall and the double doors to the delivery room opened.

Gretchen kissed Brigit's cheek. "I'll pray."

Brigit nodded, her teeth clenched, as her mother-in-law disappeared into the family waiting room. She moved her hands from their position clutching the metal bed rail to now shield her eyes from the blinding light emitted by the huge lamps over the delivery table. She shivered. It was freezing in the room.

A scrub nurse stuck her head through the exit of the sink alcove. "Dr. Shapiro is scrubbing in. He'll be here in just a minute."

Tears trickled down Brigit's cheeks. "I…want…want Will. Can you t-try to call him, again?"

A sudden draft of air filled the room as the double doors opened once more.

Her heart raced as she raised up on her elbows and turned in their direction. She collapsed with relief as Will scurried through the door, pulling on scrubs over his clothes.

"I'm here, my love!" Will slid around the table, planted a kiss on her forehead, and took his place at her side. "Now if I can just remember what the Lamaze coach taught us, we'll get through this with flying colors."

Brigit closed her eyes. *Thank you, God. If our baby is healthy, our lives will be complete.* Peace settled over her like a warm blanket. Her husband and her Lord would see her through this. She thought about the verses from her Bible study lesson: *I am with you always. I will never leave you or forsake you.*

"I was just about to start calling friends when I saw your note. I can't believe I made it here in time. I hit all the traffic lights just right. And from the looks of it, I didn't have any time to spare."

Brigit grabbed Will's hand, clasping his fingers until she thought she might break them. When she felt another contraction, she looked to him for encouragement. He put his forehead to hers and panted along with her until the pain subsided. Then, according to plan, he held up the small stuffed bear Brigit had purchased from the mall on that first shopping day. They had planned to use it for their first baby, but now it was the object Brigit had chosen to focus on during the delivery of their second child.

A nurse followed the doctor, attempting to tie the back of his surgical gown as he strode into the room. He took his place at the end of the table. "Natural childbirth. I like your spunk, gal. Let's get this show on the road."

———◆———

Will rushed into the family waiting room to join his mother. His smile held the whole story. "I'm proud to announce that we have an 8 lb. 6 oz. healthy baby. Mother and son are doing fine." More than fine, actually. They were both perfect.

Life was on the upturn once more. A healthy baby was his reward for apologizing to his mother, being a good neighbor, and serving his community.

Gretchen gave him a tight hug and then pulled back to look into his eyes. "A boy! I am so happy for you both. Now, are you finally going to tell me what you are going to name him?"

"What else? James Maxwell, after Dad—but we're going to call him Max." His eyes rimmed with tears. His name would be a daily reminder to Will of the father who had been taken from him at such a young age—a man whose smile would never fade from his memory. *Will Max look like him?*

"Thank you, Will. It's such an honor—I'm sure it would please him very much."

"If we should have a second boy, he'll be named for Brigit's father."

"And, if it's a girl?"

"In that case, we'll just have to wait and see. Anyway, for now there's just Max. Let's go over to the nursery and meet your grandson. Shall we?"

He draped his arm around his mother's shoulder as they hurried down the expansive corridor toward the nursery. They rounded the corner just as Nancy pushed Brigit's wheelchair up to the nursery window. Will kissed Brigit's lips and Gretchen clasped her hand. All three turned their attention toward the pediatric nurse as she bathed the squalling baby.

"Oh, no! I thought all babies liked baths, didn't you Will?" Brigit looked as radiant as the day he'd proposed. That seemed a lifetime ago…

Will's head began to spin. Brigit's voice sounded far away. His son's red face and quivering body were all he remembered as his world became fuzzy.

"Nancy, help, he's fainting!"

He was vaguely aware of Nancy grabbing a wheelchair from the alcove adjacent to the nursery and sliding it underneath him. He tried to follow her directions.

"Put your head between your knees. Now, breathe deep. Big inhale."

He cocked his head when he heard her chuckle.

"Reality usually sets in about bath time. You'd be surprised how many daddies we lose like this!"

———————

On an unexpectedly humid Friday night, Brigit took a seat next to Gretchen and Kelley in the third row behind home plate. "I didn't think I was going to make it. Of all days for Max to take a four hour nap." She handed the baby over to his grandmother and waved at Will, who was up to bat. It was the final game of the season and she would have hated to miss it.

"How's Grandma's little man, huh?" Gretchen held Max at arm's length and then brought him up to her face, smothering him with kisses as he patted her cheeks with his pudgy hands.

Derf slid onto the bench beside Brigit and gently pinched the baby's plump cheeks. "He's sure growing. Only a couple of months old, and he already looks like he could join the team."

"Five months old," Brigit corrected. She nodded toward the dug-out. "Are you playing today?"

He popped up from his seat with a sheepish grin. "Oops! Gotta go warm up. Only four guys in front of me."

Will hit a fly ball into the stands, ran to first base and on toward second, where he stopped.

Brigit shouted for him and continued to cheer for the "Apache Team" as batter after batter collected runs on the scoreboard. When

Derf took his turn at bat, his explosive hit over the fence and out of the park brought in both him and Raul. Derf showed off, just as he had in high school, by sliding into home.

"Auuugh!" Derf's sudden scream brought everyone in the stands to their feet.

The manager rushed to the plate, bending over him as he rolled in the fine dirt. "Someone call an ambulance!"

"I'll be right back." Brigit rushed past Gretchen and made her way through the crowd and around the backstop to where Derf lay, moaning. She knelt down beside him, pulled off her cardigan, and put it under his head.

He grimaced. "My leg! It felt like it rotated. Then I heard it *crack*. I think it just—snapped in two!"

Kelley, her husband, Jim; Pastor Paul from Derf's church, and two ladies from the Friday Bible Study group formed a circle around Derf. Gretchen rushed to join them, as the pastor helped Brigit to her feet and into the circle. They all lowered their heads and the pastor prayed. "Father God, we ask you to grant Derf freedom from pain. We pray this injury will not be serious. Please give the doctors the knowledge and skill necessary to treat him. Amen."

As Brigit turned to look for the ambulance, Will caught her arm and twirled her around. His face was red and he gritted his teeth before he spoke. "What have you been up to? How do you know all these people?"

———◆———

Will hopped out of the Mustang, uprooted another event sign from the side of the road and tossed it into the trunk. He enjoyed volunteering with the Special Olympics. It had been a long day, but the camaraderie and sheer joy on the children's faces was worth getting up so early on a Saturday morning.

Today's event was the culmination of a month-long commitment to help with the local kids. He'd been involved with all aspects of the program, from overseeing practices, organizing the advertising campaign, and then assisting with the setup and management of the live event. The kids were amazing and had such heart. Even though he was tired as he headed home, he was already starting to think of ideas to improve things for next year.

He pulled the Mustang into the circular drive, parking in front of the paved sidewalk. He jogged up to the door, leaned his shoulder against it, and nudged it open. Each time he used this entrance, it reminded him of just how much work he still needed to do—realign this door, paint the trim...

Brigit was sitting at the kitchen table, folding diapers and bibs when he came through the door. He drew in a deep breath. "Smells like you've been baking." He pulled out a chair and plopped down opposite her.

"Just a little something for later." Brigit's eyes avoided Will's. "How did the Olympics go?"

"Great. Everyone seemed to have the time of their lives."

"And you went by to see Derf, afterward?"

"No, but I called. He's got a spiral break. They've got an orthopedic specialist coming in tomorrow to look at the x-rays and examine him. They gave him painkillers and he's zonked out, so there's no reason to go down there."

Brigit glanced in his direction and nodded. "Okay."

"I think you know how upset I was last night. And all day I've been thinking about what went on at the game. I've calmed down some, so I think now's as good a time as any for us to talk about that touching scene I witnessed on the field. I want to know what's been going on behind my back. The truth." He stared at her, his jaw set, waiting for an answer.

She folded the last bib and put it aside. She cleared her throat as her eyes at last met his. "I've been talking to your mother about God...and I've been going to Kelley's Bible Study."

Will jumped up from his chair, ran his fingers through his hair, and whirled back to face her. "I don't understand this. Why? Why?"

Brigit gulped. "I really don't blame you for reacting this way. This ruse has gone on long enough." She took in a deep breath. "I guess it started with the loss of the baby. I felt to blame...like I must have done something to cause it...to happen. I realized deep inside I just couldn't completely forgive myself until I received forgiveness *from God*." She blinked away her tears.

"Brig, you did nothing to need forgiveness for—"

She sniffled, her eyes half-hidden behind a handful of tissues. "Maybe not, but that's how I felt. I thought if God would forgive me, then surely I'd be able to forgive myself."

"So, all these months, you've been lying to me."

"In a way, yes," she stammered, her eyes now flooded with tears.

Will shook his head. "You don't think God is against *lying*, then, I guess."

She looked out the window at the darkened sky. A whirlwind caught a cluster of leaves, lifted them skyward, and then left them behind as it traveled down the road and out of sight. "No. Lying is a sin. I know it—and I'm sorry for it—but I just didn't want you to be mad at me or stop me from learning about Him."

Will's face turned hot. "So, I'm the bad guy in all of this. Is that the way you see it?"

"No...I just knew you wouldn't like it." Brigit's soft voice trailed off.

"Well, you've got that right. We talked about this when we first met. I remember it very clearly." He raised his shoulders, waiting for confirmation of his memory.

"Yes, I know we did. But, Will, I've already learned so much. He's a God of love! He *does* care about us. He wants the best for us." She reached out to take Will's hand, but he jerked away.

"Tell me this, Brig. Was having our child stillborn the best for us?"

Brigit's tears resurfaced. "No, of—course n-n-not."

He put his index finger underneath her chin and lifted her head up so that her eyes met his. "Then, I think you've been duped. My mother and the rest of them—no matter how well-meaning—have twisted your mind into believing a bunch of lies."

She stood, put her arms around Will, clinging to him as she sobbed. "You just don't understand, Will. Our child is in heaven." She drew a ragged breath. "I want to see him one day. I want to spend eternity with Jesus."

He hated to see her cry. He couldn't stand it when she lost control. Most of all, he didn't want to be the cause of it. He stroked her hair. "Brig, you're getting yourself all worked up and you're not making any sense. Listen, if God is real, and knows our hearts, then He knows we're good people. He sees when we donate to worthy causes, help our neighbors, and things like that. We're good parents. We don't break the law. We're ahead of the game. You need to calm down."

She pulled away, looking up at him with puffy eyelids. "What—are y-you saying, Will?"

He closed his eyes, thinking of similar conversations he'd had with his mother over the years. Brigit was being just as difficult as she had been. "I'm telling you this God-stuff is messing with your head, your common sense. I want you to put this out of your mind. Before long, you'll see that you'll feel much better and you'll see things a lot differently."

"I don't know about that. I'm not sure I want to turn my ba-back on God."

"Brig, you've got this all wrong. You wouldn't be turning your back on Him. You'd only be living your life the way we agreed we would. We don't need Christians or the Bible to dictate things to us. We're intelligent. College graduates. We can figure all of this out for ourselves." He kissed the top of her head, then her cheek.

Brigit frowned, but then nodded "I'm still going to pray, though Will... still talk to God. And, I don't w-want to give up my friendship with Kelley and Gretchen."

He looked down at the floor. "If you don't let those things interfere with our lives, I guess that's okay. But let them know, in no uncertain terms, that we are going to live our own lives. If you don't, we're going to end up arguing all the time and that won't do either of us any good. And, it certainly won't be any good for our child."

Her voice was soft, almost a whisper. "Our children."

Will shook his head and frowned. "Sure, our 'children'—someday."

"No, our children. Plural. About seven months from now." She walked over to the counter and lifted the cover off the cake pan. Underneath was a pineapple-upside down cake. This time, the rattle was on top.

———◆———

"Mind if we come in?" Brigit raised her eyebrows in her mother-in-law's direction.

"Of course, dear, and have a seat. I was just perking a fresh pot of coffee. It should be done any minute." Gretchen lifted the baby out of Brigit's arms. "How's Max, today, huh?"

Max blew his customary bubbles and reached out to snag Gretchen's glasses.

She rescued them just in time and laid them on top of her Bible on the counter. She headed toward the kitchen and sat down at the table with him on her lap. "Look what Grandma's got for you." She placed a soft green bear in his hands.

Brigit followed her into the homey room. "I know it's not our usual day to get together, but I wanted to stop by with some news."

"About Derf? What did the specialist have to say?"

"He has a painful spiral break. I'm afraid he's going to be laid up for a while."

"That's too bad. I'll try to stop by and see him later this afternoon." Gretchen turned Max around to face her. She held onto his wrists, and pulled the palms of his hands together, forming a pat-a-cake. "Has Will been over there, yet?"

Brigit folded her hands and rested them on the table. "Not, yet."

Gretchen raised her eyebrows." Why not?"

"He's talked to him on the phone, but he's kind of upset with Derf—and me, and you—the whole world, I guess."

"He saw all of us praying on the field, didn't he?"

"Yes. He thinks I've been deceiving him—which I have. And, now, he wants me to stop all this 'God nonsense' as he calls it. He wants things back like they were. He says the sooner I get over all of this, the sooner life will get back to normal for us."

"Is that what you think? Is it what you *want,* Brigit?"

She bit her lower lip. "I want Will to be happy. If I can be a Christian in my heart, then—"

Gretchen put her hand over Brigit's. "I can try to talk to him, if you'd like."

She shook her head. "No. You two have just mended your broken relationship. If you try to defend me—or God—it would only revert things back to the way they were before. I don't want that for either of you." She gave Gretchen's hand a squeeze and then walked toward the coffee pot.

"I understand. And I won't mention to Will that you stopped by. But I will pray about this, dear."

"Thank you." Brigit looked up at her with a slow smile. "I knew you would." She took a coffee mug from the cupboard and held it out toward Gretchen. "Can I pour you a cup?"

"Please. For some reason I didn't want one earlier. Then, just a few minutes before you knocked on the door, I felt like having one." She winked at Brigit.

Brigit nodded her head. She had come to love and trust her mother-in-law. She already thought of her as a blessing in her life, and a very dear friend. She might no longer attend Bible Study, but there was still a lot she could learn over a cup of coffee.

Lord, please help Will's friendship with Derf endure this. But, more than that, help it to grow even stronger and use it to speak to Will's heart. Amen.

She set the coffee mugs on the table, watching Max—now asleep in his grandmother's arms. They certainly hadn't planned for another baby so soon. She was only just now bonding with Max. But she recalled what Kelley had written on the card attached to her shower gift: *A baby is a gift from God...one of life's greatest blessings.*

"By the way, Gretchen, remember that news I said I wanted to share with you?"

CHAPTER 12

———◆———

DARBY CLAIRE, NAMED FOR BRIGIT'S paternal grandmother, was born seven months later. Just two years following her birth, Will marveled at the fact that today they would be celebrating Max's third birthday. Where had the time gone? Perhaps all parents felt that way when they realized their lives with their children were compressed between two events: birth and high school graduation.

His career at the newspaper had skyrocketed. The added responsibilities, followed by a series of raises, put them in a better financial position than ever. They had been able to take a family vacation to Disneyland and purchase a new car for Brigit

Both Will and Brigit loved being parents. They doted on their children. They made friends with several other couples with young families and enjoyed getting together with them often. Their lives were dominated by outdoor activities, sports, and community involvement.

A strong breeze coming down the mountains lifted Will's Stetson off his head as he walked down the circular driveway. It was a Christmas gift from Brigit to replace the previous hat he'd purchased at a thrift store. It was a nice thought, but he still kept the old one. Wearing it reminded him of where he'd been and just how much he'd accomplished in such a short time.

He brushed the red dirt off the rim of the hat and hustled to the back of Neil Hawkins's horse trailer. "Good to see you, Neil." He drummed his fingers against the metal doors as he waited for Neil to let down the tailgate.

Brigit sauntered from the house, shielding her eyes from the afternoon sun with one hand, holding onto little Max's hand with the other. When they got close, Max squirmed loose of her grasp and ran toward his father.

Will winked at Neil, then scooped the boy into his arms and twirled him around. "What do you think is in this trailer, Son?"

"My horsey!" Max squealed, his pink cheeks lifted by his broad smile.

"You peeked!" Will showered him with kisses while Brigit tickled him. "Happy birthday!"

"So, you're three years old, now. Is that right?" Neil called from inside the trailer.

Max wriggled down from Will's arms and ran to the bottom of the ramp, looking up at Neil. "Today's my birfday." He used the fingers of one hand to help three fingers from the other one to stand straight and tall.

"Well, happy birthday, Max. Now, stand back and take a good look at this big fella." The lanky cowboy, who had been Jim Hayes's best friend, led the brown and white horse down the ramp and onto the hard packed earth. He lifted Max into the saddle and led the horse, fourteen hands tall, into the newly built corral on the west side of the house.

Will intertwined his arms around Brigit's waist as they watched their son have his first ride. Will pulled his hat lower on his forehead to shade his eyes from the intensity of the sun. "We really appreciate you doing this for Max. We won't forget your kindness."

"I was glad to do it. Your father would have done the same for my grandson." He led the horse up to Will. "Want to give this a try?"

"Sure." As Will took the reins, he looked up at Max sitting tall in the saddle.

"Mommy and I have one more surprise for you." He grabbed a small red cowboy hat from the fencepost and placed it on his head.

"Look, Mommy. I'm a real cowboy!" Max smiled in her direction as she snapped a series of pictures.

———

While Max took a nap, and Will visited with Neil outside, Brigit worked at preparing food for the party. She put Darby in her booster seat, filling a tray with finger foods to keep her occupied. She was two years old and could feed herself, but she was a lot messier than Brigit remembered Max being at this age.

They had invited Gretchen, and three families that were their closest friends for a cowboy barbecue. She shook her head. Why had she insisted on making all of the dishes herself, leaving her no time to spare in her busy afternoon?

As she pulled the cake out of the oven, her eyes traveled past the big kitchen island to admire the tooled leather sofa and loveseat. When they first moved there, they didn't have much furniture—and Will's mother had helped them with the home's down payment—but as Will's income rose, they had replaced their old furnishings with a number of new southwestern pieces.

She no longer worked at the hospital. Her health had been somewhat fragile since Darby's birth. Nothing serious. But, still, the opportunity to be home with the children during these formative years was one she grabbed without hesitation.

Following Kelley's suggestion to plant a garden, she'd become more interested in eating healthy. So she spent time preparing dishes using fresh vegetables, reading about nutrients, and chasing off wild rabbits that found the green leaves of her plants irresistible.

They were happy here in Apache Junction. Will played cowboy on the weekends, finding it a great way to relax from the daily grind of newspaper life during the long workweek.

Living in the vast open spaces of the east valley was a dream come true. Both she and Will loved living near the Superstitions. The sky was clear and the mountains were spectacular in varying shades of grays, pinks, and purples.

Brigit turned her face toward Will as he entered the kitchen and planted a kiss on her cheek. She wiped sweet potatoes off Darby's nose, neck, and hands, then lifted her into her father's waiting arms.

Her chubby hands reached for his hat.

He was quicker than he had been the day before, when she had imprinted it with green beans and carrots. He nuzzled her soft cheek. "This has been quite a day for Max. He sure loves that horse. He insists his name is Big Fella, like Neil referred to him."

Brigit stood and wound her arms around Will's waist. "If the party goes well, I'll say we've had a successful day." She reached around Darby to give him a gentle kiss.

He shot her a broad smile. "He was so excited, I'm surprised you got him to come in, let alone agree to go down for a nap."

"He was really tired after that long ride. I'm only going to let him sleep for about an hour, though. If he naps too long, he'll wake up crabby for his party." Brigit ran a wet dishcloth over the vegetable-strewn table. "Could you change Miss D's diaper and put her down for her nap while I clean up here and take a shower?"

"On my way." Will lifted Darby onto his shoulders, giving her a horsey ride of her own down the long hallway toward the bathroom.

Brigit walked in the opposite direction, toward the master bedroom and bath. Within minutes, the warmth of the shower poured over her sore body. She and Will had been taking riding lessons for the past month in anticipation of teaching Max to ride his new horse. She would soon be twenty-seven. She should be in better shape than this. Her lower back screamed in pain every night. And, although he denied it, she suspected Will was hurting, too. Yesterday, she'd caught a glimpse of him massaging his back as he got out of the car.

She loved her children, but really appreciated times like this when the house was quiet. She wished she could lie down and rest for a while, too, but the cake still needed to be frosted. She toweled off, grabbed her robe from the hook opposite the shower and headed toward the kitchen.

Max's door was open as she walked by. He wasn't in his bed. She checked the bathroom next to it, but no Max. Maybe the birthday boy was too excited to sleep.

Will was standing on the patio drinking a tall glass of iced tea when she joined him. Following her sketch, he had hung the crepe paper streamers according to plan, but a wind had come up and some of them were already floating off into the distance.

She looked up at the menacing clouds forming on the horizon. "I hope it doesn't rain. Much as we need it, the party is what's important, today. Hey, do you know where Max is? He's not in his room."

Will grabbed at an orange streamer as it took flight. "Maybe he's playing with his Legos."

Brigit cupped her hands against the window and peered inside. The tub of multi-colored Legos sat untouched in the family room. Her eyes drifted over to the corral.

Her heart skipped a beat and her breath quickened as she discovered Max had somehow scaled the fence and was inside with Big Fella. "Will! Come quick!" She ran off the patio, almost tripping over the Big Wheel abandoned in the front yard. Although her heart beat wildly, she tried to keep her voice calm as she called out to Max. "Stop! You can't be in there, honey. It's dangerous!"

Her pulse raced. *Be calm. Don't panic.* The rest happened in slow motion: Big Fella's mane blowing in the wind...the rattler coming out from under a nearby bush...the horse rearing...Max's arms flailing as hooves trampled him underfoot...his small body lying crumpled on the hard earth...

Will rushed past her to grab his son's limp body and race for the car. The tires screeched as he rode the Mustang down the dirt road and onto the paved county highway, a cloud of dust trailing behind.

All too-familiar tears smeared Brigit's face. She attempted to brush them away as the grit enveloped her. She collapsed onto the ground. "God, please help us!"

———◆———

Sweat beaded on Will's face as he pushed the gas pedal to the floorboard. He divided his attention between Max's still body and the busy traffic on the road ahead. While his son's life hung in the balance, dozens of trucks pulling boats—beds piled with grills, tents, and camping equipment—clogged up the main road out of Apache Junction.

He beat the palm of his hand against his steering wheel and laid on the horn. His mind whirled with fragmented recollections of the last fifteen minutes. One moment he was sipping iced tea and hanging decorations, the next he was running to the car with Max in his arms.

He turned the wheel abruptly and swung the Mustang off the pavement and onto the soft dirt of the shoulder. When it started to fishtail, he slowed down enough to straighten it out, motioning to the driver on his right that he needed to cut between him and the car in front. He fumbled to roll down his window and yelled, "My kid's hurt. I've got to get him to the hospital!"

The driver slowed enough to let him in.

Seeing no traffic in the oncoming lane, Will pulled into it and accelerated. Several miles later, he crossed into the city of Mesa and headed for the only hospital for miles around, not far from the dry bed of the Salt River.

When Max started to convulse, he knew he had made the right decision not to try to drive to Brigit's former hospital in Tempe. He stopped the car at the emergency entrance to the Mesa Community Hospital, engine still running, and scooped up Max. He half-ran, half-stumbled to the triage desk. "Help! Somebody, please help!"

———◆———

Brigit sat on the edge of the chair alongside Max's bed, holding his small hand between both of hers. By the time she had left Darby with Gretchen and joined Will at the hospital, Max was already on life support. She watched as the respirator moved up and down, sending needed oxygen into the lungs of their beautiful little boy.

Knowing it was an accident didn't ease the pain. The old familiar feelings she had experienced following their first baby's death hit her again like a blast of cold air. She shuddered as they threatened to drag her back down to the pit of denial...the wasteland of despair. She remembered it only too well.

Where was God when she needed Him? Wasn't He supposed to keep her family safe? Didn't the Bible say He came to heal the sick and brokenhearted?

She had risked everything—Will's trust—by sneaking behind his back to attend those morning Bible studies with Kelley. And, what about Gretchen and those long mid-week visits so she could spend more time with her grandchildren? Weren't they really Brigit's way of concealing her real purpose—to learn more about Him?

She had asked God for a happy, healthy family...a stable marriage... financial security. She had poured herself into a pursuit of "holiness" only to have this happen. Even if God didn't *cause* it, surely He could have *prevented* it.

Hello, darkness, my old friend. I've come to talk to you again.

———◆———

Day after day, for a full week, Will and Brigit stayed by Max's bedside. Will held his hands, talked to him—even sang him songs—while Brigit stood by the window, looking outside at the heat rising from the pavement of the parking lot two floors below and mumbling to herself.

Gretchen came by every day, as did Kelley and Derf. Their visits were always cut short by Will's tirades. He was unwilling to have them pray by his son's bedside, his flat-out rudeness fueled by anger at "The Almighty."

On Saturday night, one week after the accident, the doctor advised them to turn off the machine. Will listened as the doctor explained such terms as "brain dead" and "prolonged assisted breathing." His thoughts and emotions tangled in his mind, a jumbled mess—an impossible choice—which in the end, Brigit relinquished to him.

Again, their lives had been turned upside down. Again, their relationship would be put to the test. Would Will face things alone, again, while Brigit retreated deeper and deeper into herself?

Fresh tears collected on the stubble of his unshaven beard. He nodded to the doctor and grabbed for Brigit's hand, holding it so tightly that her fingers turned white. Minutes later, as their freckle-faced son took his last breaths, Will lashed out at God. "We haven't done anything to you, but you've taken *everything* from us!"

Would he ever be able to fill the void that already threatened to swallow him up?

———◆———

Four days later, in the aftermath of an afternoon dust storm, Will sat on the bench opposite Max's grave. His little boy who dreamed of being an astronaut and a football player, his child who would climb in bed with his little sister and comfort her during a rainstorm, had lost the battle. Now Will and Brigit had to make it through this dark time for Darby's sake.

A hand fell on Will's shoulder. He looked up to see Pastor Childers from his mother's church. He had spoken at Max's funeral the day before. Will had agreed to let the guy officiate. After all, he reasoned, what could it hurt?

"Mind if I sit with you a bit?" He stood in front of him, his shoes dusty and his salt-and-pepper hair disheveled.

Will put his hand out to cover the bench. "I don't want to be rude, Pastor, but I *do* mind. Your speech at the funeral is where I draw the line. I don't want you coming around and pushing all this God stuff on us. We used to be content letting God be God and having Him leave us alone so we could be us. But a lot has changed over the course of our marriage. You might say that for some reason God hates us—and the feeling is mutual."

The pastor put a hand on Will's shoulder. "I'm sure God doesn't hate you, Mr. Hayes."

Will shrugged the unwanted gesture away. "Oh, really? Well that's what it seems like to us. How does He treat people that He *really hates?*" Will rose from his seat, to his full height of six feet, towering a good six inches over the balding clergyman.

The pastor took a step backward. "His very essence is *love.*"

Will's entire body shook. "Well, excuse me if my wife and I find that hard to believe. We don't feel singled out, though. Oh, no. We see it in our neighborhood and on the news. We see it in our family. Guess what? The love of Christ you talk about? It doesn't exist."

I can't believe the audacity of that guy. Who is he to lecture me? He has no idea what we've been through. Will stood and turned to leave, bringing his clenched fist down hard on Max's gravestone, a carved likeness of a child in the arms of Jesus. "My mother is likely responsible for this. I'll have it replaced."

———◆———

Will turned into the driveway and killed the motor. Neil's horse trailer was parked by the corral. He was glad to see Neil had come so quickly, but he was still fired up from his talk with the reverend. He closed his eyes and took in a deep breath before he opened the car door.

Neil was already out of his truck. "This wasn't the horse's fault, Will." He opened the gate, placed a rope around Big Fella's neck, and led him into the horse trailer, shutting the doors with a *clang.*

Will shook Neil's hand. "I know it's not, Neil. God did this to our son. No one else to blame but Him." He clenched and unclenched his fists.

Neil frowned, hesitating before he spoke. "You really feel that way, don't you, Will?"

He felt the heat rising from his chest to his neck and upward to his cheeks. "How else would you expect me to feel? We've lost two children in almost five years. God has it in for us."

"There are a lot of people in this world who've had tragedies in their lives. God isn't to blame for all of their troubles." Neil's voice was soft, but firm. "Get a grip, son. God doesn't set out to hurt people. God is——" He put out his hand to pat Will's shoulder, but recoiled when Will jerked away.

"Don't say it. I've heard it all before. Just go on and get out of here with that animal. Donate him. Sell him. I don't really care what you do with him just so long as I don't have to see him ever again." Will turned his back on Neil and stomped toward the corral.

He lifted the small saddle off the fence and threw it into the powdery dirt. Then, he grabbed a sledgehammer and swung it against the rough sawn boards. He'd soon have the fences down, but he knew the memories of his little boy's first and only ride would remain a part of his life forever.

———

Brigit watched as Neil's truck pulled onto the main road, letting the curtains fall back into place before putting Darby down for a nap and walking outside. She grasped the edges of her long skirt with both hands to keep it from blowing in the strong breeze.

From the way Will was attacking the corral, his visit to the cemetery must have brought him more pain than comfort. He glanced up at her as her shadow fell across ground, but he just shook his head and continued to swing. "You just have no idea how hard it is…to be beaten down at every turn…over and over again…day after rotten day…year after year."

Brigit turned an empty bucket upside down and took a seat. Her shoulders shook as she cried. *I have no idea how hard it is? Who does he think he's talking to?* Yesterday, he bagged up Max's clothes and hauled them off to Goodwill. Today, he was destroying the fence that he'd taken such pride in building. She'd hidden the photo album at Kelley's—and it would remain there—at least until his fury subsided.

She'd been angry at God, too, initially. But, her belief in His goodness—His faithfulness—had won out. He had poured the light of His love into her soul as she prayed in the hospital. She was comforted by His words as she read them in the Bible, uplifted by the prayers of the many friends that cared about her and Will.

This was the "valley of the shadow of death" in the Twenty-third Psalm. But, she would get through it because God was walking this road with her. He'd walk it with Will, too, if he'd only let Him…

As the last board toppled to the ground, Will opened his hand and released the hammer. He turned, collapsing near her feet, and dropped his head into her lap.

She removed his hat and laid it on the discarded saddle. Her fingers trembled as she stroked his wet hair. Why wouldn't he let God comfort him? Why was Will's heart so hard?

CHAPTER 13

———•———

HIS FINGER WAS POISED TO snap a picture of Darby with ice cream on her chin.

She grinned at him, and then licked it off with her tongue before he could get the shot.

Will sighed and set the camera on the table. It was her fourth birthday. She was a golden-haired charmer with a great sense of humor—and she had him wrapped around her little finger.

Weekly grief counseling had helped them all to cope better, but they were still not ready to throw a big birthday party. Instead, they had taken her to their favorite neighborhood ice cream parlor for a low-key celebration—just the three of them. He collapsed into the booth next to Brigit, drained of all the energy he had left in him on a weeknight. "I'm tired. It's been a long day and it's almost her bedtime."

Brigit wrinkled her nose. "It's only seven o'clock." She ran a napkin across the table, absorbing some of the melted chocolate, and added it to the soiled pile on the tray.

Will grunted as he rose. He took Darby's hand and led her out to the car, placing her in her booster seat.

Brigit took over, buckling their daughter in with practiced ease. "Want me to drive?"

Will shook his head and slid into the driver's seat. Once the key was in the ignition, he backed out onto the street. He'd be fine once he got some sleep. He'd had a week full of nothing but deadlines to meet. He'd stayed up late, more than once, to finish writing his column. The job was getting to be sheer drudgery. He daydreamed of their upcoming Hawaiian vacation in June. *One more month and sandy beaches, here we come.*

"Will!" Brigit grabbed the steering wheel and gave it a sharp jerk to the right in order to avoid an oncoming truck. "Pull over right now. I'm going to drive. You haven't got your mind on the road and you're going to get us all killed!"

The *click* of Brigit's seat belt releasing was the last sound Will heard before everything turned black. When he came to, he was in the hospital emergency room, hooked up to a heart monitor. He watched as feet hustled back and forth outside the privacy curtain. *What was going on?*

He felt dizzy and nauseous. He closed his eyes, waiting for the feeling to subside. He willed his breathing to slow. As he relaxed, someone approached his bedside.

"Let this be a sign to you...a message. Read what it says, Will." The stranger's voice was calm, but firm.

Will didn't need to look. He knew this place only too well. "My son, Max, died on his third birthday. This is his grave."

The stranger shook his head. "You're mistaken, Will. Read the inscription."

Will stared at the black marble head stone in front of them displaying the words *"James William 'Will' Hayes. Loved by his wife, children, and his creator—whom he rejected."*

He woke with a start, panting and struggling for breath. The alarm on the monitor sounded, loud and ominous. A petite nurse in blue scrubs threw the curtain back in response. She found Will's pulse and gave her attention to her watch as she counted. "Must have malfunctioned. It happens all the time."

"Why am I in the Emergency Room? Where's my wife?" Will asked, struggling to shake the hold the dream had on him and return to reality. *He was driving. Had they been in an accident? Were Brigit and Darby all right?* He shivered.

"I'm your nurse this morning. My name is Jennifer. You're here because you blacked out while driving a vehicle, as I understand it. I think your wife went to your mother's with your daughter. She said she'd hurry right back. In the meantime, we're going to complete some tests so we can get you out of here. Sound good?"

Brigit and Darby were okay. Will sighed in relief. "We weren't in accident?"

"Didn't sound like it."

"I'm grateful for that." Will ran the palm of his hand over his mouth.

The nurse helped Will into a wheelchair, pushing him down the hall past medical equipment and gurneys parked off to the side. "Your wife filled out your medical information and gave consent for further medical testing." The nurse slapped a button on the wall, opening double doors labeled, "X-Ray."

———

It was still dark out the following morning when Will and Brigit headed across town during rush hour traffic to the new high rise medical complex for a before-hours appointment with their primary care physician. "The emergency room doctor said I most likely had a virus. I don't understand why Dr. Williams would need to talk with us about that." He wrinkled his brow as he followed Brigit through the revolving door of the four-story glass and steel building. He braced himself for the worst. After all, two things doctors seldom did nowadays were house calls and extended hours.

Brigit grabbed his hand, swinging it back and forth as they walked. "They did a lot of tests. He probably got the results this morning and wanted to go over them with us before he starts his rounds at the hospital. I'm sure everything is fine."

When Will rapped softly on the leaded glass window, Dr. Williams unlocked the door and led them through the darkened waiting room and into his private office. The light from his desk lamp cast ominous shadows on the walls. Will's mouth went dry.

"Have a seat, you two. I haven't seen you in a coon's age. How long's it been, anyway?" The silver-haired doctor put on his lab coat and straightened his tie before he sat down at the large oak desk across from them.

"Two years…since Max died." Brigit's hands trembled as she searched in her purse for a tissue.

"How have you two been managing?" The doctor asked without looking up from the folder bulging with papers in front of him.

"We've been having a rough time of it, so recently we started going to counseling. I think it's beginning to make a difference. We're just now learning to talk to each other…to say the words, you know." Will loosened his tie. It was stifling in the small office. He needed some fresh air.

"Let's take a look at these lab results, shall we? See what we've got and what we're going to do about it."

Will's heart began to race as the doctor flipped through page after page. The silence was agonizing. He had the feeling that the next words the doctor spoke would change his life forever.

Dr. Williams finally looked up, removed his glasses, and let his eyes meet Will's. "We'll have to order a few more tests, but let's cut to the chase about what we've learned so far. And that is, according to these preliminary findings—and they're just preliminary, mind you—you may have pancreatic cancer."

Will drew in a quick breath and reached for Brigit's hand. "What? I don't think I heard you right." He turned to look at Brigit. Her face was pale, tears forming in her eyes.

"Here's what we know. You've been tired a lot lately. You've lacked a normal appetite for quite some time, accounting for the sudden and unexplained loss of weight. You mentioned abdominal pain, especially when you lean forward putting on your shoes, for example. Your blood and urine testing show the sudden onset of diabetes, in spite of the fact that you have no family history of the disease." The doctor looked Will directly in the eyes. "Correct?"

"In retrospect, I've had some symptoms that told me *something* was wrong, but I've just had so much on my mind..." Will stood, placed his hands on the desk, and hung his head. "So, what's the bottom line, here, Doc? I mean, it sounds serious."

"I'll be straight with you, Will. It *is* serious. We'll need to send you to an oncologist—Dr. Brahms is one of the best—so I'll try to get you an appointment to see him this afternoon—"

Feeling lightheaded, Will fell back into his chair. His voice was barely audible. "Today? So soon?" He tried to recall when the first symptoms had started.

Dr. Matt Williams ran his hands through his thinning gray hair. "This is an aggressive form of cancer and if it's as far along as I think it is, we have no time to waste getting treatment started. We'll do all we can but, of course, things are ultimately in the hands of God."

———————

Once back in the parking lot, Brigit sat woodenly as Will beat his fists against the dashboard of the aging Mustang. Her thoughts swirled. *Will might die...*

"God's hands," he yelled, "God's hands! I refuse to be put in *God's* hands!" His knuckles turned white as he clenched his fingers into a fist.

Brigit laid her hand on Will's shoulder. "Maybe we should talk to your mother, or her pastor. Maybe we should—"

Will flinched. "Are you kidding me? Our lives are a shambles. How much more proof do you need that God is just who I said He was all along?"

Would Will have enough fight in him to face the long battle ahead? Brigit's mind drifted to the New Testament hidden in the bottom drawer of her dresser.

Brigit gripped the steering wheel. "Listen, how about going for a drive over to the university and taking a walk to our favorite spot? Maybe grab something at The Chuckbox? Just like old times."

Will stared out the window. "The walk sounds good, but I don't think I could eat a thing."

"Let's just play it by ear once we get there." Brigit forced a smile and turned the key in the ignition. This wouldn't be anything like the old times when they'd first met. And, she wasn't so sure that reminders of brighter days were what either of them needed right now. She was only certain of one thing: this time she was going to depend on someone bigger, wiser, and stronger than herself to see this through. She could only pray that Will would learn to do the same.

As she eased the car onto the freeway, she surveyed the smog hanging over the Phoenix skyline, much like the dark cloud hanging over her family. She didn't understand why two people so perfectly matched, who made each other happy in so many ways, would continue to face obstacle after obstacle in their lives together. Hadn't they been through enough?

Her cheeks were soon wet with tears. She tried to swallow the lump in her throat. Her mind returned to the all too familiar dark thoughts she'd faced when Max was on life support. If this doctor—this oncologist—couldn't work a miracle, the love—and the light—of her life might soon be extinguished.

But she and Darby wouldn't be left to face the dark times alone.

———————

Thirty minutes later, they left the car in a parking lot and walked down the university mall to the campus library. "We haven't been back here since we got married." Brigit smiled when Will raised her hand to his lips and kissed it softly. She thought about their wedding day...how beautiful it had been; how much had happened since then. Their sixth anniversary was coming up. Would they spend it together?

"We said we were going to revisit the cactus garden every year on our anniversary, but we never did." Will's prominent Adam's apple trembled as he swallowed.

"No, we never did—until now." A lone tear trickled down Brigit's cheek, instantly drying in the mid-morning heat.

Will stopped walking, turned, and searched her face. "When we first met, we thought we had the world by the tail, didn't we?"

Brenda C. Poulos

"I suppose so…we really didn't have any reason to think that our future together wouldn't be as bright as this Arizona sun." Brigit extended her hands high overhead, rising onto her toes for emphasis.

Will shook his head. "Little did we know that—" A catch in his throat caused him to pause. He took in a deep breath and held it.

Brigit forced a smile, grabbed his hand, and started walking once more. "You know, the counselor said negative talk wouldn't get us anywhere."

"Ah, but 'Miss Only Think Happy Thoughts,' you can't go through life deluding yourself, either. Things are just how they are. We've got to face the facts."

Brigit's voice turned solemn. "All right, and just what are 'the facts'?"

"Well, as I see it, they are: One. I have cancer. Two. It's in an advanced state because I didn't notice the signs, or I denied them for far too long—the latter is probably the truth—and Three. I'm going to fight this thing as long as I can because I don't want to leave you and Darby. Four. I need to get things in order because I have a feeling it's not going to be easy. And five. You need to prepare yourself—and Darby—for a future only the two of you may share." Will bit his lower lip.

She felt paralyzed by his bluntness. He had said the words so matter-of-factly, she almost felt ill. She struggled to hold it together for his sake, taking in a deep breath. "Here's our bench. Let's sit a few minutes." Brigit looked up at the Ocotillo in full bloom. It was somewhat larger but just as beautiful as it had been the day they first met.

"I came hurrying around the corner, over there." Will pointed in the direction of the Language and Literature Building. "And, I froze to the spot when I saw you sitting here." He raised Brigit's chin, looking at her as if seeing her for the first time. "I fell in love with you at first sight. But, I love you more now than I knew possible that morning." He kissed her tenderly, tears from both of their eyes, intermingling and falling together onto their clutched hands.

"I love you, too, Will." She'd always love him. Nothing would ever change that. But, death would separate them forever...

He rubbed his eyes with the back of his hand and forced a smile. "If love is enough, we'll get through this and our marriage will be even stronger than it is today."

"And what if love isn't enough? What will happen to us, then?"

———◆———

Will lay still as the MRI machine began its full body scan later that afternoon. In their preconference, Dr. Brahms had confirmed the diagnosis and he was confident that the cancer had spread. The MRI would pinpoint just where and to what degree. It would disclose whether there would still be a chance for treatment or whether the window of opportunity had already passed.

Will supposed Brigit was lost in her own thoughts as she waited for the test to conclude. He dreaded that she'd cope with this news as she had in the past, by retreating into her shell and letting old fears once again take up residence.

Dr. Brahms had shown them pictures of the organs most likely involved, drawing a jagged red line over them to indicate the most likely path the cancer would take. The timeline he had penciled in next to it was graphic enough, too. This certainly was a doctor who believed in taking the direct approach. But Will appreciated the fact that Dr. Sol Brahms was straightforward, sharing the truth, no matter how hard it was for them to accept.

As the *whir* of the machine faded and he was released from its clutches, Will wanted nothing more than to go home for a nap and wake to a different reality—that this day had only been a bad dream. His blood chilled as he walked into the waiting room and saw Brigit, deep in conversation with Derf. *Why had she called him?*

"Here's Will now." Brigit jumped from her seat, giving Will a hug before he sat in the empty chair by Derf.

"Hey, Buddy, good to see you." Derf clapped him on the back. "Brigit was just filling me in on your diagnosis. That's rough. Really rough." He gave Will's shoulders a squeeze.

"Yeah. That's one way of putting it." Why was he feeling such anger toward his friend who had obviously rushed over after work to be with them? Why was something always happening to *them,* while Derf, Kelley, and all of their other friends seemed to go through life unscathed?

"My broken leg is nothing compared to what you two have gone through—are going through. I hope you know if it were possible, I'd trade places with you." Derf's eyes were filled with compassion and love.

"You really mean that, don't you? Most people would just give a sigh of relief that it wasn't them, but you…you…I just don't understand you. It's like saying you'd die for me, you know?" Will's throat tightened. He closed his eyes and leaned forward, resting his elbows on his legs and letting his head fall into his cupped hands.

"I have no fear of death, Will. None at all. I'd hate to leave Tammy and my parents, of course, but if it would give you more time to—" Derf grunted, adjusting his position in his chair, his jaw twitching.

Will raised his head to turn and look into Derf's eyes. "Go ahead and say it. I know what you're thinking. I know what Brigit's thinking."

Derf's face paled. "And what's that, Will?"

Will scanned the room full of cancer patients and their families. How many of them were going to trust their own instincts? How many of them would put their faith in God? And, if they did, would it be because they *really believed* or would it be because they had nothing else to hang on to...to put their hope in? Did they feel like him? Up against a wall, trapped in a room with no door, wanting to run, but finding no way out?

He looked toward his friend. He needed to keep his distance from him. Derf had a way a making him feel it was all right to be dependent, to rely on someone else—God to be explicit—for the strength to face what was ahead. But he'd show Derf, and his wife, that he could beat this thing. And he'd prove to them, once and for all, what a hoax and a fraud God really was.

His eyes met Derf's, his steady gaze taking in his dark hair and deep brown eyes for the last time. Then, he leaned over and whispered in his ear. "I can't allow you to poison my mind. I want you gone when I get back." He turned and walked down the hall leading to the terrace, a blast of heat hitting his face as he walked out into the sweltering Arizona afternoon.

Brigit reached over and took his hand in hers. She caressed it, brought it to her lips, and placed the gentlest of kisses on his palm. Her tears flowed freely.

Will slid his arm over her shoulders and pulled her close. He was ashamed that he'd yelled at her after Derf had left. He was sorry he'd been rude to Derf, too. What had gotten into him, anyway? The very people trying to comfort him had been caught off guard by his hateful attitude. It was God he wanted to lash out against; they had just been in the way.

Will glanced at his watch. Five forty-five. He couldn't concentrate on the paperback novel in his hand. He had read and reread the same line for the last five minutes. The activity in the crowded waiting room was beginning to get to him. He closed his eyes. It dawned on him that he was younger than his own father had been when he had died. Darby would likely grow up without her father, too. *I'm so sorry, honey. Daddy's so sorry.*

"Mr. and Mrs. Hayes." A somewhat rotund nurse with green eyes and a bulging clipboard waited as Brigit gathered her purse and Will tossed the book into his briefcase. The hallway leading to Dr. Brahms private office was colder than Will remembered it being when they'd arrived hours earlier.

It was now nearly 6:00. He gazed back at the filled waiting room… some of them looked hopeful…some discouraged. Heaven? Hell? Eternal slumber? How many believed God would heal them?

How many believed He even cared?

CHAPTER 14

———

LEAVING WILL IN ROOM 208, Brigit stopped briefly at home and then drove toward her mother-in-law's rambling 2,500 square foot house. Gretchen admitted that it was too large for her, but she wasn't ready to give up the memories it held of her happy life with Will's father—days when their family was still together.

When Brigit pulled into the driveway, the side door of the house opened and Darby skipped down the steps. "Where were you, Mommy? Grandma was getting ready to call you again. Why didn't Daddy come to pick me up?"

Darby's voice agitated her. It had been the longest day of Brigit's life and at eight-thirty in the evening, she was in no mood to be reprimanded by a four-year-old. She peeled herself from the bucket seat, shook her head, and drew in a deep breath before grabbing Darby's Hello Kitty suitcase from the backseat. "Let me come in and talk to Grandma a minute and I'll explain things." She put her hand on Darby's back and prodded her to where Gretchen stood, holding the door open for them.

Darby turned around to face her mother. "Why did you bring my suitcase? I can go home with you, can't I?"

Brigit gave an extra-long hug to her mother-in-law. *This is going to break her heart. God, please help me relay this news to Gretchen in the best way possible.*

"Darby and I have already eaten. Have you had dinner, dear?" Gretchen motioned toward the dining room table where two of four place settings still waited. "There's still plenty left. I can reheat it for you."

Brigit walked into the welcoming room. Delicate white placemats, linen napkins, flickering candles. At one time, these special touches Gretchen provided for their weekly dinner would have made her smile, but tonight they sent a shudder through her. "No, I'm not hungry. I'm sorry. I didn't even think to call you. We've had a really long day and I was hoping that I could leave Darby here tonight, and you could get her off to preschool in the morning. I went by the house and got her some clean clothes." She trailed her hand across the top of Will's favorite chair.

"Mommy!" Darby stamped her foot, a second irritation for Brigit.

She bit her tongue. Every action—every word of tonight's conversation—would prove meaningful in how they all dealt with the news she was about to share. She forced a calming breath. After receiving Gretchen's assenting nod, she bent down and took Darby by the shoulders. "I want you to take this bag and your suitcase upstairs, put your pajamas on, and hop into bed. I'll be there in a little while, after I talk to Grandma."

"But—"

"I brought your library book. "You can look at the pictures while you wait for me."

"Mommy!"

"Now, go!" Brigit raised her voice, immediately regretting that it caused Darby to cry.

Darby's jaw dropped, tears welling up in her eyes. After pausing for a moment to stare at Brigit, she ran up the stairs, dragging her pink suitcase behind her. *Thump, thump, thump.* She slammed the bedroom door, shaking the family pictures on the staircase wall.

Brigit closed her eyes. *She's sensing my frustration. I need to keep it together for her sake.* She struggled against the temptation to run to her. Will's mother was expecting to hear what had happened.

Gretchen set a steaming mug of hot apple cider on the side table in the living room. "You're scaring me, Brigit. Sit down and tell me what's wrong."

She glanced at the closed door at the top of the stairs before sitting at the small glass-topped tea table. "I left Will at the hospital. He's going to have surgery tomorrow morning." *Please, God, give me the right words to say. This is his mother.*

Gretchen gasped. "I knew something was wrong when you called me to pick up Darby from preschool. Seems I'm always the last to know." Her dark eyes looked accusingly at Brigit.

She reached over to give Gretchen's hand a firm squeeze. "I'm sorry you feel that way, but we only found out about this a couple of hours ago. We met with the doctor early this morning, and Will had test after test, all day long. Then, we met with an oncologist late this afternoon—" She buried her face in her hands, sobbing.

"Oncologist?" Gretchen moved over to stroke Brigit's hair, and then gave her a tissue.

Brigit's shaking hands dabbed at her eyes. "This is the kind of news no mother should have to hear. I wanted to wait to talk with you in person—"

"Then tell me, honey, please." Gretchen's hands twisted in her lap.

Brigit paused a moment, then squared her shoulders and blurted out, "Will has an aggressive form of pancreatic cancer. They're hopeful a large part of it can be removed, if we act quickly. We were fortunate there was an opening in the surgery schedule for tomorrow morning. We snapped it up without giving it a second thought. I don't mind telling you, we're both scared."

Gretchen's face paled. "No. Please, God. No!" She closed her eyes, tears trickling down her once-rosy cheeks. She wiped them away with her trembling fingertips, took a deep breath, and then headed for the phone. "I'll call the prayer team. We'll start praying right away."

"Wait a minute." Brigit patted the chair her mother-in-law had just vacated. "Come sit down. I have a question about prayer I'd like to ask you." She chewed at her bottom lip.

Gretchen hurried back to sit opposite Brigit, looking at her with bloodshot eyes and forcing a half-smile. "I've faced this before. God saw me through it. We must have faith that He will be here with us... taking care of us...just as He was when Jim was ill." She reached out to give Brigit's hand a squeeze. "Now, what would you like to know, dear?"

Brigit folded and unfolded her napkin on the table. Her lips quivered when she began to speak. "Do you think, even though Will doesn't want anything to do with God, that God might still answer our prayers for his healing?"

"Dear—"

"Will just isn't ready to give control of his life over to God, yet. He's been angry for so long, he just doesn't know how to let it go. There's no talking to him about it. His heart is so *hard*." She closed her eyes and hung her head.

"The Bible tells us that God hears and answers prayers according to His will. We don't know what the answer will be, but we do know that He works the circumstances of life out to fulfill His ultimate purpose for us and for all of His creation." With a quick kiss on the top of Brigit's head, she headed for the phone.

Brigit followed Gretchen into the hallway. God had certainly blessed Brigit when he gave her Gretchen—a special mother-in-law and friend. Her heart warmed as she thought about the many prayers that would soon go out in Will's behalf. As she blew her nose, she looked up through blurred eyes to see Darby standing at the top of the stairs.

———————

Late the following afternoon, Brigit answered the soft knock at the door of Will's hospital room.

Gretchen gave her a quick hug before walking toward the bed. She pulled up a chair and sat down on the edge of it. Her slender fingers reached through the bedrails to grasp Will's hand and study his face before speaking. "His color's good."

"Yes, it is." Brigit followed, straightening the sheet and pulling the light blanket over him. "He was just given some pain medication. He's been awake, off and on, all afternoon." She glanced at the wall clock. "I must have dozed off myself. I didn't realize it was four o'clock already."

All of a sudden, Brigit was no longer able to control the built-up emotions of the day. She clung to her mother-in-law, crying—the first good cry she'd allowed herself all week. She used a crumpled tissue to dab at her tears. "I appreciate being able to leave Darby with you for so long, especially since I know you've been worried, too. How's she doing?"

"She's all settled in the children's play area down on the first floor. When I left her, she'd already found another little girl to play with. I'm so glad hospitals are starting to put in supervised childcare rooms. They give parents one less thing to worry about. Am I right?"

Brigit nodded. "The surgeon talked to me after the surgery. He said Will did fine, but that later this afternoon he should get a preliminary pathology report and he'd come in when he got it and share the results. For now, though, all we can do is wait." Brigit stroked Will's thick hair noticing, for the first time, almost imperceptible gray at the temples.

Gretchen gave Will's hand a pat before releasing it and standing. "We can do much more than that, dear. We can pray." Gretchen's fingers caressed Will's cheek.

"To tell you the truth, I don't even know what to say to God, anymore." Brigit paused and closed her eyes against more tears. Her voice shook as she continued. "What if He doesn't choose to heal Will? What if he dies?" *Did I really say that out loud?*

Gretchen winced, but then her expression softened. "Start by telling God your fears. Ask Him for the strength to get through this time and to give you the perfect words to use when you tell Darby."

"Have you said anything to her?"

"Only that her daddy is sick." She looked to Brigit. "I thought you'd want to be the one to tell her."

Brigit's lip trembled. "Oh, I do, but actually I think what you've told her so far is sufficient."

Will's silver-haired doctor, still wearing his scrubs, stood at the door. His sad eyes and drooped shoulders told the story—even before he began to speak. "I do, too."

———————

Brigit put folded laundry into the dresser drawers. At Darby's insistence, she had gathered up their things and driven home. Her little girl had sensed the seriousness of things. Maybe she would rest easier in her own bed.

Darby slipped into her pajamas and then sat cross-legged on the floor, facing her mother. "I don't know why I didn't get to see Daddy, today. I wanted to look at his stitches. And why couldn't he come home tonight?" Her lower lip protruded in an exaggerated pout.

She motioned for Darby to sit on the bed and then she sat down beside her on the pale pink bedspread. She stroked her strawberry-blond hair and drew her close for a long hug. "Daddy's operation this morning made his tummy sore. He's resting. In a day or two, he'll be home. Then, you can talk to him all you want. I promise." She pulled back, searching her daughter's eyes for a hint of understanding.

"Jason Bender's mommy went into the hospital and she *never* came home." Darby fell into Brigit's arms, sobbing.

Brigit clutched Darby's head to her chest, sharing her sadness as she cried tears of her own. Her eyes fell on the "Adorable Pets" calendar pinned to the wall. *I hope I don't regret this later, but I've got to do something to get this kid's mind off of Will and asking all these questions. I just don't have any answers.* "I have a surprise for you."

"What is it, Mama? Will I like it?" She clapped her hands together, jumping up and down. "When will—"

"Darby, please! Mommy's got a headache." Brigit stood and closed the top dresser drawer, running her hand across its smooth edge. She had stripped and sanded it herself, painting it a creamy off-white. Gretchen's artistic touch, layering the delicate pink and yellow roses and trailing vines, had been the perfect complement to its curved lines. "I'm sorry, pumpkin. I didn't mean to snap at you." Brigit turned around to tickle Darby's ribs and plant a kiss on her forehead.

"What's the surprise, Mommy?" She placed the tip of her nose next to Brigit's so their foreheads touched.

"I talked with the lady at the pet store and she said she'd give me a good deal, if I'd buy *both* of the puppies we saw last week. So, if you'd still like them, and will promise to be a good helper by making sure they have food and water, then we can go to the mall on Saturday and pick them up." Brigit winced. She should have checked with Will before saying anything. She'd just felt so desperate to end Darby's constant chatter.

Darby pushed herself up onto her knees and then stood, bouncing on her bed and laughing. "Yes. Yes. *Two* puppies. Wow! Can I call Grandma?"

———◆———

Will lay under the light blue afghan his mother had given him the morning following his surgery. She loved to crochet and was often making blankets for shut-ins at her church. His hand ran over the soft strands. *I need to let her know just how much I appreciate all the things she's done for us: meals, watching our little girl, her unending love and support.*

"Scooter and Mike? Did I hear you right?" Will called from the sofa as two white fluff balls, chased by Darby, slid across the kitchen floor. *So much has changed in just two days.*

"Mommy let me name them. They're both girls." Darby twirled, princess-style with her arms open wide, across the open floor. "I just love them so much, don't you?" She stepped closer to him, a smile on her face, but with brows drawn together.

"Please, Will, can we keep them?" Brigit crossed her fingers.

His scowl faded, replaced by a genuine smile. "Are you sure about this, Darby girl? You'll have to do your part in caring for them."

Darby skipped over to the sofa. "Daddy, please." She placed the palms of her hands on his cheeks and pressed inward, making his lips pucker.

"I guess it will be all right. They'll have to sleep in your room, though. I've been in the hospital for two days and only home for a few minutes. The doctor says I need to rest, so I can't have puppies waking me up in the middle of the night."

"Thank you, Daddy!" She planted a sloppy kiss on his cheek and ran down the hall. "I already made beds for them next to mine."

I bet you did. He turned toward Brigit, tears moistening his eyes. "I don't want to leave her. I don't want to leave either of you." He turned over and patted a place beside him on the sofa.

She smiled. "I guess the dishes can wait." She lay on her side, facing him on the narrow outside edge of the sofa, heart-to-heart—'modified spooning'—Grandpa called it.

He brushed a stray hair away from her eyes and then buried his nose in the silken strands. He inhaled the scent he had become so accustomed to over the years—orange blossoms in the spring, cinnamon and vanilla in the fall. "The doctor bills are going to mount up fast and insurance is only going to pay part of them. So I'm thinking we should sell the house and move back into town."

Brigit pulled back, tilting her chin. "Move? But—"

"We could rent something inexpensive. Something with a smaller yard would be easier to take care of." He gulped down his feelings of defeat. At one time, owning an acre of land was a matter of pride. Now, it was a visual reminder that soon he would no longer be able to keep up with the mortgage, or the maintenance, of his own home. "What do you think?" He raised his eyebrows. He hoped she'd see this move as a practical decision and not as a sign that he was giving up the fight. Their beautiful home deserved to be taken care of and enjoyed by a growing family.

Brigit moved off the sofa to sit facing him on the floor. She pondered aloud. "Hmm…I guess if we move closer to the hospital, I can work part time in the fall when Darby starts kindergarten."

Will twisted a curl of her hair around his finger and smiled as it bounced back when he let it go. "You know, we moved here with a dream of riding and ranching, but it doesn't seem like that is going to work out." He cleared his throat and pasted on a smile. "It's time we face our new reality—whatever that ends up looking like. Maybe if we move, we can get past the dreams of *what might have been* and face whatever lies ahead."

———

Will closed his eyes as Brigit drove home following the first chemo treatment. He wanted nothing more than to go to bed and rest, but only halfway home, he suddenly felt ill. "Brig, can you pull into a gas station?" The car had barely stopped when he ran for the restroom.

He got as far as the sink before he vomited. Rinsing it out with water, he caught a glimpse of himself in the mirror. *So, this is what it's going to be like. My eyes are already black underneath. It won't be long until everyone at work will be asking me if this is more serious than I admitted. Then later, if I have to take a leave of absence, how will I be able to tell them everything without falling apart?*

When he exited the restroom, he found Brigit waiting for him by the cash register, browsing through bumper stickers. He'd never been a fan of them, but as Brigit began to read some and laugh, he was drawn in. Soon, he was by her side, chuckling along with her. And, before he knew it, he was making his purchase. "I Believe in Life BEFORE Death!" *I intend to live that sentiment to the fullest.* He smiled as they walked to the car.

They would have to cancel the Hawaii trip, but when he was through with chemo, maybe they'd rent a van and travel up north to the Grand Canyon, then west to Yosemite, ending up in Lake Tahoe to visit with Ken Martin, an old friend from college. Darby and his little girl were nearly the same age.

It would be a family trip of a lifetime—a kaleidoscope of memories for his wife and daughter to treasure.

———•———

Three weeks later, Will was sitting at the kitchen table, filling out an official-looking paper when Brigit came through the door. "How did it go?"

She put the small cardboard box on the counter, collapsed into a padded dining room chair, and kicked off her shoes. "It was fine. There are a dozen or so cards and notes in the top of the box from your co-workers. They were sorry not to see *you*. That reminds me. They even had a cake. I saved you what was left. I need to get it out of the car before the icing melts."

He scratched his head, wincing at the sudden pain it caused his tender scalp. Would he ever get used to the fact that he no longer had a thick head of hair? "Maybe I should have gone, but I just didn't want all of them looking at me and telling me they hoped I'd be back to work, soon. You and I both know it's going to be months before that happens." *If ever...*

She walked toward the door, but then turned abruptly back toward him. "I don't want you to talk like that anymore. You need to think positive thoughts and—"

"So that's it. I thought you were kind of late. You've been at the library again, haven't you?" He drummed his fingers on the table as he waited for her response.

She slid back into her chair and grabbed his hand. "You can find a lot of useful information at the library. I may be a nurse, but we don't have to blindly agree with everything the doctors say, you know. There are other approaches to cancer treatment that might be effective as supplements to chemo. We just have to keep an open mind."

He stretched his arms upward toward the ceiling and then let them fall onto the table. "Like what?"

"Okay. There's nutritional therapy and aromatherapy for starters. And—"

Will rolled his eyes, then interrupted. "Come on. I've always taken vitamins and we eat well. Where's that gotten me? And you'll have a hard time convincing me that smelling things will cure diseases."

"Well, I've got to do *something*. Don't you realize how helpless I feel?" Her face reddened. She lowered her voice and mumbled under her breath. "I can't just sit around and think dark thoughts all day like you do."

"What? You think I just sit around? You know what I'm doing right now? Here, look at this; then tell me about dark thoughts." He tossed a paper in her direction.

Her eyes widened. "Advanced Directive?"

"I'm sure you're familiar with it, being a nurse." Defensive. Sarcastic. This wasn't the old Will.

She gulped. "Yes. But—"

"And, how about this? A 'Do Not Resuscitate' order. And, the big one: my will." He pounded his fist on the table. "Sitting around? I don't think so."

———

The house sold within two weeks to a guy who owned a local moving company. Within a month, he had helped Will and Brigit move into a house within walking distance of their first apartment, just a few blocks from Kelley and Jim.

Will understood that Brigit wanted to live near her best friend, but it still made him uncomfortable. However, she had come home so excited to find something to rent within their new budget that he didn't have the heart to refuse.

The first month of chemo had been rough, but now, three weeks into the second round and the introduction of a new drug, Will often slept on a pallet near the bathroom. Nauseous, and plagued with bouts of vertigo, he found himself unable to concentrate long enough to read. An occasional football game on television was his only diversion.

"I'll call you on my lunch break." Brigit walked down the hallway and picked up her keys. "It's Thursday, you know. There's the weekly dinner at your mom's tonight. I'll pick up Darby after school, take her to the dentist for her checkup, and then swing by here to get you about 5:00."

"If I'm not too tired." He clicked the television on and fell back into his recliner.

Brigit sighed, and then paused before she spoke. "You need to make the effort, Will. We've had this night with her as long as I can remember, and we should keep going as long as you're able. You know she wants to see you."

"But, do I have to go *there?* I mean, I'm not going to eat anything anyway. Nothing tastes good anymore. Can't she just drive over here? Now that we've moved back into town, it's a short drive for her." *It's an effort just to get dressed anymore.*

"True. But she doesn't like to drive at night. And she loves to cook for us. It gives her something positive to do. You know how it is."

He hesitated. "Call me around noon and I'll let you know how I feel."

"Okay." She threw him a kiss and took a sweater from the hall closet. "Darby, come give Daddy a hug and let's get going."

Darby skidded around the corner and grabbed onto Will's arm. "I have something for you, Daddy. I made you a picture." She thrust a colorful crayon drawing into his hand and ran for the door. "I hope you like it."

"I do, honey. It's great." His heart sank as she headed out the door.

The car started and the garage door closed, signaling their exit.

Tears filled Will's eyes as he studied Darby's gift—a crude drawing of him in bed, sleeping, while Brigit and Darby stood by his side, giant tears forming a puddle at their feet.

The house was quiet. Boxes yet to be unpacked filled the small living room. He had resolved to help Brigit out by straightening up the kitchen and washing the sink full of dishes, but decided he'd take a short nap first. He was slowly making his way toward the bedroom when the doorbell rang. He froze in the hallway, no intention of answering the door. When the bell rang again, he crept toward the door, looking out the peephole.

A guy with a Bible tucked under his arm slid a pamphlet through the mail slot, and then walked down the cracked sidewalk toward the house next door.

Will continued down the hall, falling sideways onto the bed, chilled but without the strength to pull the blanket up around his shoulders. *Why can't they simply leave people alone? Let them believe or not believe in whatever and whomever they want.*

CHAPTER 15

———————————

Rushing into his mother's house that evening, Will dispensed with the formality of holding the door open for Brigit and Darby. The dentist had been running late, so they had made it home to pick him up with only minutes to spare. These dinners were always timed to be hot and on the table at 6:00 p.m. Being late was one of his mother's pet peeves.

Will paused. Not so long ago, the smell of her homemade chicken and dumplings would have made his mouth water. But today it hit him in the gut, making his stomach turn. He just hoped he could keep it together for an hour or so. After all, he'd missed dinner last week...

"Son, it's so good to see you. I'm glad you felt up to coming tonight." She kissed his cheek and gave it a gentle pinch between her thumb and forefinger.

She hadn't done anything like that since his little league baseball days. He winked in response, just like he'd done back then. "It's always good to see Grandma, isn't it Darby?"

"Yes. I see her after preschool every day. She's helping me with writing my name and counting all the way to one hundred." Darby exchanged huge grins with her grandmother.

"My goodness. I had no idea you were learning all that from Grandma." He felt a familiar sinking feeling in the pit of his stomach.

Someone other than himself was teaching his daughter the basics. He wished he had more energy—and more time.

"We appreciate everything you've done for us, Gretchen." Brigit added, en route to hang their sweaters in the hallway closet.

"I enjoy having Darby spend time with me. I guess you'd say it works out for both of us." She handed the silverware to her granddaughter and nodded toward the Dining room.

Will looked out the large picture window at the spacious backyard. Some of the plants were already budding out. It was the first of March. The last one he'd ever enjoy.

At his appointment yesterday morning, Dr. Brahms had estimated he had about three months to live. It had been a shock to both he and Brigit, even though they were expecting the doctor to say something about the effectiveness of the chemo. It was just that when he said it—straight out like that—it took them both aback. They'd managed to hold it together in the office, but when they reached the car, they'd both broken down.

The reality of his death had hit both of them full force. Unable to speak—inept at finding the words—they had just held each other and cried.

He hadn't been able to conceive that their life together would soon be over—that their dreams wouldn't be realized. The importance of the things they'd accomplished together faded into the background. All he'd been able to think of was Brigit and Darby and how they'd be forced to navigate the future alone.

When no more tears would come, he had reached up to wipe the tears from Brigit's cheeks. "Let's try to focus on something positive, huh?"

She had nodded. "Like what?"

"Let's move up the date for our family trip. Now that I won't be taking chemo any longer, I should feel like traveling a bit. If you'll do the driving, I'll ride shotgun with the map. We'll show Darby how to take pictures and make her the official historian." The memories of the trip would have to last Brigit and Darby for a long time to come—his parting gift to them.

Darby pulled on the sleeve of his shirt. "Daddy, are you day dreaming, again?"

"I guess I was." He bent down to kiss her cheek, and then turned to his mother. "Mom, would you mind if we all crowded around the kitchen table tonight? I was just thinking about the good times we've had around this table and, well, I'd just like to eat in here tonight. That's all." He had started to say *one last time*, but stopped himself.

His mother gave him a long look, and swallowed hard before fishing a tissue out of her apron pocket and blotting her eyes. She turned her back to him and placed her hands on the countertop for support. Her shoulders shook. "Sure. That'd be fine." Her voice hitched, sounding small when she finally answered. "Can you set the table in here, Darby girl?"

Will crossed the space between them and placed his arms around his mother, holding her tight as she sobbed. She could read between the lines. She knew what he was saying.

"Just who do you think you are, anyway? God?" Will hissed at Jim, interrupting his neighbor's attempt to "share the gospel" with him the Sunday afternoon before their family trip.

Jim rang the doorbell during the second half of the preseason football game. Will tried to control his irritation by asking if he minded coming back later—like maybe in a year or so—but Jim had just smiled and pushed past him, taking a seat in *his* recliner. He said he didn't mind waiting until the fourth quarter ended. To top it off, he helped himself to the last chicken wing.

Will always watched the post-game analysis, but wanted Jim out of there as quickly as possible, so he clicked the television off when the game ended. "So, what prompted you to come over here on a *Sunday afternoon?*" Just because Brigit was thrilled to be living back in the "old neighborhood" near Kelley, didn't mean Will was glad to be in close proximity to the influence of the Jamisons.

Jim's face lit up, ready to be heard after a thirty-minute fourth quarter plus overtime. He cleared his throat. "I just thought I'd come over and chat with you before you take off on your big trip." His face grew somber as he spoke. The corner of his lip twitched as he slipped an envelope out of the pocket of his blazer and handed it to Will.

"What's this all about?" Will put his forefinger under the flap, tore the envelope open, and wiggled the card out. It had a picture of a dove and an open Bible on the front. Without opening it, Will tapped it against his knee. He didn't need a syrupy card filled with biblical senti-ments. His blood was boiling. This was going to be brutal.

Why couldn't people leave their religion at the door? Why did they think they needed to challenge everyone else's beliefs? Why couldn't Jim just let him lead his own life? No harm. No foul.

Kelley's mother had died on New Year's Day. Maybe he could throw him off by asking about her. "How are you all doing since Claudia's death?"

Jim ran his tongue along his teeth. "It's been a few months, but I don't mind telling you, it's been hard on all of us."

"You guys are Christians, right? I've heard that you all rejoice when people pass on to their 'heavenly reward.' So what's the problem?"

"Kelley's mom *wasn't* a believer." Jim slipped a small New Testament out of his shirt pocket and opened it at the place he'd marked with a slip of paper.

When Will saw a tear form in Jim's eye, he regretted what he'd said, in spite of the fact that he'd interrupted his game. "Oh?"

"She didn't go to Heaven, according to the Bible. I'm here because I care about you and your family. I don't want to see that happening to you." He opened the book at the place he'd marked, his eyes scanning the page to find the verse he wanted.

"Don't worry. It's not your concern. Anyway, I don't believe in Heaven—or Hell for that matter."

"They're real places, Will. The Bible talks about them. It's a fact you need to face, *this* side of death." Jim took in a deep breath, ready to read aloud.

"So, Brigit told you about the prognosis?" He tried to control his sudden anger. Where did Brigit come off talking to their neighbor about Will's health? It was none of their business. And, it wasn't Brigit's story to tell.

"She did, in fact. She—" Jim stopped talking when Will cut him off.

"You talked to Brigit? About me?" He glared at Jim, and then threw the card down on the coffee table. She'd already shared the privileged information so he'd be more than justified in shutting down Jim's unwanted visit.

"Yes. She's worried about you. She said she's tried to share the gospel with you several times, but you haven't been receptive to hear about God's plan of salvation."

"You're darn right! Where do you get off trying to push your beliefs onto everyone in the neighborhood? Judging us. Just who do you think you are, anyway? God?" He marched to the living room and stayed there, with the door open, tapping his foot.

Jim hoisted himself out of the recliner and walked in his direction. "Listen, I didn't mean to make you uncomfortable. It's just that—" His eyes were misty. He shook his head, and then looked down at his dusty loafers.

Will put his hands on Jim's shoulders and gave him a slight push in the direction of his house before closing the door.

———————

A month later, Will, Brigit, and Darby took to the road. The first three days of their trip were even more wonderful than Brigit had imagined. The Grand Canyon was truly spectacular in April. A mist hung over the cliffs, shrouding them in mystery unlike what they had seen in travel catalogs. And even Yosemite was more breathtaking than she had expected.

"Mama, pull over, I want to get a picture of that deer." Darby rolled down the window, ready to take the shot as Brigit pulled the rented VW van to the side of the road.

Brigit shivered at the blast of cold air. "Be quick about it. The rain has started again, and we don't want any of us to get wet." She put the afghan back around Will's shoulders. He had been dozing a lot this morning and coughing in his sleep, in stark contrast to the boundless energy he seemed to have had at the beginning of the trip.

As Brigit pulled back onto the roadway, she noticed a sign advertising a clinic a mile ahead. Since Will's breathing had become a bit labored, she decided to be on the safe side and have someone at the clinic check his lungs. She was a nurse, but dealing with bronchitis on the road would be a bit scary. Home with his own doctor would be the best place for him if her suspicions were confirmed.

An hour later, Brigit had followed the doctor's instructions and cancelled the last leg of their trip. As they headed back toward Arizona, Will developed a bad cough. Brigit worried about what life would bring them in the next few days. *Dear God, I can't drive, worry about Will, and keep it together for our little girl all at the same time. You say you manifest your strength in our time of weakness. Please be my strength right now. Please get us safely home and give Will yet another opportunity to accept the forgiveness you promise in your Word.*

By the time they got home, Will had severe pain in his chest. Brigit drove him directly to the emergency room. Following a five-minute examination, and a pneumonia diagnosis, he was admitted to the hospital. Even though she was exhausted by the long drive, she knew there was something else she needed to do—call Gretchen.

She prayed for Will as Darby lay stretched out next to her on the waiting room bench, sleeping. She was peacefully unaware of the magnitude of the situation and Brigit was grateful for that. She was also thankful they had been able to experience the family time the trip had provided, even though it was much shorter than they had planned.

"Mrs. Hayes, you can go in, now. He's asking for you both." The nurse waited as Brigit picked up Darby and then led them down the wide corridor to a room in the ICU. One wall was completely glass, showcasing the bright oranges of the desert sunset and lighting up the western sky.

Brigit laid Darby in a chair, draping her sweater across her legs. She walked toward the bed and grasped Will's hand. "How are you feeling?" She stroked his cheek before giving him a gentle kiss.

His voice was barely a whisper. "They started IV antibiotics. The nurse said by tomorrow, I should notice a big improvement."

"Is it okay with you if I take Darby over to Gretchen's? I can bring her back tomorrow or the next day, after you've both been able to get some rest."

His eyes drifted in Darby's direction, watching her chest raise and lower as she slept. "Take Darby, but stay with her and get a little nap, yourself. You've been driving for two days straight. If you want, send Mom over here to be with me. You can switch places in the morning."

"That's a good idea. I'll get us something to eat on the way to Gretchen's and we'll see you tomorrow." She massaged his temples until his eyes fluttered shut. She felt the sudden urge to pray once more before she left. She kneeled by his bedside. "Great and merciful God, I ask for healing for Will's body, but also for his soul. You know all things, Lord. You know if this pneumonia will take his life or if it will be the cancer. I am asking you to give us more time…but please don't let him suffer. Amen."

"Daddy, are you going to-to die?" Darby asked the next day, her expressive eyes filled with sadness. She'd be five years old at the end of next month.

Will wanted nothing more than to be her Prince Charming at her Cinderella party, but that wouldn't be possible, now. "I might, pumpkin." *I knew this day would come. I practiced what to say, but now I'm not so sure…*

Darby laid her head on his chest, clinging to him and sobbing. "I don't want you to die, Daddy."

Her tears soaked into his hospital gown, saturating his very soul. He stroked her hair. "I love you, Darby."

"I love you, too, Daddy." She wiped her eyes on the sleeve of her Grand Canyon t-shirt. "Will you go to live in heaven, then?"

He struggled to speak over the loud whir of the oxygen machine. "I-I-"

Brigit turned her attention from her Bible. A stubborn lock of brown hair fell in front of her face, partially hiding the dark shadows under her eyes. She shifted in the chair opposite the door, tucking her bare feet under her denim skirt.

Will knit his eyebrows together, a plea for help.

Brigit shook her head.

She must be confused by his hesitation. After all, he'd rejected God, so why not emphatically state the truth, as he saw it, to Darby? He guessed it was because the hard- line approach hadn't worked so well with Brigit. Why repeat the same mistake with their daughter?

Brigit went back to reading her Bible. He had finally come to terms with her defection to the other side. They each had their own decisions to make. If Christianity was what gave her comfort, as she had said to him earlier in the day, what was the harm?

"I think there *might* be a-a—special place, call it heaven, if you like. But, Darby, it would be for *really* extraordinarily good people like— Billy Graham—or Mother Theresa."

"Who?" Darby scrunched her face and glanced toward Brigit.

Brigit looked up from her reading, giving Darby her full attention. "Sweetie, you probably don't know who they are. Most people would say they're examples of very good people. They live unselfish lives and do lots of nice things for others."

Darby turned back toward Will. "But, Mommy's going to go to heaven, Daddy. Don't you want to go there, too?"

Will closed his eyes, focusing on breathing. He was thankful that Brigit had helped him out with that explanation, but it was clear she'd already been doing some talking with Darby on the subject. He didn't like it, but he felt too tired and too weak to make an issue of it now. It was an effort to talk...to stay awake. "Daddy's just going to float away on a big, white, fluffy cloud. It sounds peaceful, doesn't it? Being up there with birds, butterflies, and rainbows?" He forced himself to open his eyes, giving Darby his best effort at a convincing smile.

Darby was still staring at him. "I suppose...And what about, you know, that *other* place?" Her big green eyes looked up at him, expectant.

"Oh," he said. "I know the place you're talking about." His mind drifted for a moment, to a vision of fire and anguished faces...a movie he'd seen several years before.

Darby ran her finger gently down the I.V. tubing toward the site where the needle was inserted into the back of his hand. "Well, Daddy?"

"Sweetie, I don't think hell is a *real* place. It's just a figment of someone's overactive imagination to scare people into being good. You don't fret about it, all right?" He stroked her silken hair, then pinched her dimpled cheek. He wasn't worrying, so why should his little girl? He'd figured this heaven/hell thing out a long time ago. He knew what would happen when he died. He'd just float away into blissful nothing-ness—billowy clouds and blue skies—into a dream world of his own choosing.

Darby leaned over and put her nose next to his, moving it back and forth—a butterfly kiss they had shared every day since her birth—but this time she ended the ritual by gently pressing something into the palm of his hand.

———•———

CHAPTER 16

A WEEK AFTER BEING ADMITTED to the hospital, Will was moved to the palliative care unit—the goal being to keep him as comfortable as possible in his last hours. He looked at the oxygen machine. If it weren't for its presence, he'd have thought he was in a nice hotel room.

It had finally come down to this, after nearly a year of being carted back and forth between doctors' visits, tests, and chemo regimens. After trying such unconventional therapies as naturopathic blends, aromatherapy, and acupuncture, this is where he would say his final good-byes.

The cancer had claimed his vital organs one by one, but it looked like the pneumonia would act as the final gatekeeper to his life. When the end came, he didn't want any heroic measures. He would welcome the end of his pain. He would simply drift into a deep sleep from which he would never awaken. No streets of gold, no crowns encrusted with precious jewels, no God or Jesus or Allah...

After a brief visit from his mother, Brigit, and Darby, he felt tired... so very tired. He didn't have the strength—or the will—to fight any longer. He reached over to the side table and picked up the angel pin Darby had pressed into his palm days earlier. It had once graced the collar of Brigit's wedding dress—a reminder from his mother just how great the divide was between faith in oneself and faith in God. He uncurled his fingers and let it drop onto the crisp white sheet.

He found it nearly impossible to fill his lungs with air. It felt like trying to force liquid through a bent straw. Cold sweat beaded on his upper lip and brow.

He recalled the time he had gotten locked inside an old refrigerator abandoned on the back lot of his grandparents' summer cabin. It had been dark, too, and he was soon out of air. Unable to breathe, his heart had raced. Then came the lifesaving surge of cool air when Grandad opened the door.

A nurse walked toward the bed. She placed the cold metal of a stethoscope on his chest. Was this to be the end? He started to panic. *Wait! I'm not ready. I can't do this. I...* A minute later, warmth washed through him as she injected morphine into the IV.

He relaxed, feeling back in control of himself. *Ride the waves. Just go with it.* Over and over, he repeated key phrases from the tape he had been listening to for the past week. It had been recorded by a doctor who'd become famous for helping people with terminal diseases cope with the moments preceding death. He followed the memorized instructions, envisioned himself drifting away, waving goodbye to Derf...his mother... Darby...and finally, Brigit.

As the proverbial clock struck twelve midnight, his breathing slowed, and then stopped. He relinquished his life to an uncertain future. But that great hope for the death that he'd fixated on—that release from the pain he'd been living with—didn't come.

No, this death wasn't what he'd expected. He became instantly cold. Not an exhilarating cold like that of air hitting one's face when stepping outside on a winter's morning. Instead, it was an all-consuming cold. And, it *hurt.* He shivered. *Surely someone can get me another blanket.* His screams echoed back, unheeded. On this side of death, he was utterly and completely alone.

He left the bed and retreated to the far end of the room, looking back at someone who resembled him—horrified at the pale appearance, the vacant eyes. It was his body—he was certain of it—and he was *dead*—he knew that, too.

He struggled to understand what had happened. It was as if his soul now existed on another plane outside the confines of time and space. There were two of him: one, the lifeless body remaining in the hospital bed; the other, a wavy, misshapen replica of his "old" physical body—a kind of alternate self—one still capable of thinking and feeling.

He recalled cartoons he had watched as a child, in which the spirit body lifted out of the dead person or animal, an exact replica of its physical body. The "spirit body" could walk, dance, jump, even run—it could do anything that the person's physical body had been able to do—because it *was* still flesh and bone.

He touched his right arm with his left hand. He wiggled his toes, amazed that a child's cartoon could have been so accurate.

"Follow us. Hurry. Don't delay!"

Will's groggy thoughts were interrupted by the urgent request of two aberrant figures beckoning him from the doorway of the hospital room. He shrank back at their appearance. Hollow sockets where eyes should be, gnawed fingertips.

They grabbed his arms and flung him forward. He was powerless to resist them. He had no choice but to obey.

Darkness wrapped around him, thick and damp. It squeezed him, giving off a strange oppressive vibe. It had a mind of its own, intent on devouring him.

The hair lifted on the nape of his neck. His chest tightened as he was pushed and shoved by the agitated beings.

They became more antagonistic as they traveled farther away from the hospital room. Their blackened bodies began to change, too, as healthy tissue and muscles were replaced by oozing sores and burnt flesh. They leered at him with large reddish-gold eyes and curled their lips to reveal the sharp fangs they clicked together intermittently. They gave themselves over to bouts of laughter, enjoying his distress, reveling in his screams.

More and more creatures fell in beside them. The small group swelled to a hissing throng. They chanted as they marched with stiff arms and legs, prodding him along faster and faster.

He tripped several times and was nearly trampled underneath their long, bony feet.

Their leader pointed to a platform in the distance. "There. Terminal Four." Their voices grew to a crescendo as they reached a transport of some kind, slid a door open and pushed him inside. A loud *gong* sounded as the door was shut. The deafening shouts of his tormentors grew faint as they shuffled off into the distance, their odor lingering in his nostrils.

His trembling fingers inspected the rough metal surrounding him. It was a capsule only slightly larger than he was and cold to his touch. It confined him—top, bottom, and sides all around—limiting his movements. It shook as energy built up underneath it, then thrust it upward into outer space.

A single window, directly in front of his face, provided a view of the universe as he was propelled past galaxies filled with sparkling stars and whirling planets. Like a NASA rocket, it plunged straight ahead through the universe and beyond. He was spellbound to experience such a vast and active eternity.

He continued to travel past myriad universes filled with color and light, spellbound by the beauty and the enormity of it all. Planets pulsated, luminescent stars danced in and out of intricate rainbows. Then, all of a sudden, as if the vessel had reached the boundaries of all existence, it was hurled into utter and complete darkness.

He swallowed hard. Outside of all time and space, suspended on the brink of nothingness, he experienced a familiar tightness in his chest. He squirmed. Horror partnered with fear and together they took on a ghostly shape. They became a living entity that assaulted him from within and without. Feelings, once emotions to be experienced, had morphed into actual *living* beings with form and substance.

And, they became formidable enemies.

Will clawed at the sides of the capsule. He had traveled too far away from home… his family…his friends…his *life*. How would he ever be able to find his way back? As quickly as the question formed in his mind, the answer was on its heels: *He would never return. The laws governing this transport were clear: it was a one-way trip.*

Instinctively, he reached for Brigit. She had been his rock, his constancy, his solace. But she wasn't here. His hand dropped to his side.

He strained for air that would not come. His heart pounded wildly in his chest without rhythm or purpose. How painful was this going to be? Would he be able to endure it?

Within moments, the vehicle dipped into an accelerated descent. Faster and faster it fell—so fast that he could actually *hear* the sound of it. He envisioned a gigantic magnet, an unbelievably strong force, pulling it into a downward spiral toward its final destination. He averted his eyes as a planet—an ominous white-hot fireball—opened, swallowing his vehicle with its voracious appetite.

As a boy, fishing with Granddad was Will's favorite thing to do. Seeing a fish jump out of a clear, cold lake was exhilarating. It really got his blood flowing. He remembered catching his first fish—the energy it took to reel him in, the struggle of it on his line. No matter what that fish did, he was headed straight for the frying pan.

There was nothing he could do about it.

He pounded against the sides of the capsule with his fists, but his screams were beyond anyone's hearing. He shuddered, aware he was no match for whatever lay ahead. His spirit was crushed by the inevitability of his situation.

Dread, as he'd never experienced before, gripped him like a vise. This was the end of the line. He closed his eyes, imagining who—or what—he would see when the door opened.

The wailing he heard was his own.

———————

"Out!" The order blared from overhead as his worst fears materialized.

Will pressed against the back wall of the capsule, cowering in the blackness. The air crackled with electricity, the atmosphere toxic. When he tried to breathe, a searing pain traveled from his nose to his throat. He held his breath as long as he could, but finally was forced to gulp down the sulfur-like fumes and cry out in agony as they scalded his lungs.

He smelled burning flesh and heard the cries of a vast multitude in the distance. He inched forward, his heart pounding at the sudden appearance of flames on the horizon.

Someone grabbed his arm and flung him outside. He jerked away, looking down to examine his torn flesh in the dim light. He withdrew back into the safety of the capsule, but was dragged out by two creatures similar to the ones that had come for him in the hospital. They bared their teeth and spewed endless vulgarities before finally releasing him.

Looking up, he realized there was no sky. He sensed the vastness of the cavernous space. It felt hollow, but at the same time he sensed it was occupied. He was unable to move, paralyzed by his inability to process all he saw and felt. He shuddered as he drew his knees up to his chest and huddled on the dock.

Soon, another capsule arrived, then another and another. He cried out, trampled underfoot by those exiting the transports. He trembled as the expanse pulsated, then swelled—enlarging itself to accommodate the growing numbers—assimilating each newcomer, only to swell, again and again. Each time, the shrieks of the others joined his own. The collective drone of them was deafening.

He was pushed aside with each new arrival, driven back—and down— farther and farther from the dock. He was plowed under, drowning in a sea of helpless, flailing bodies.

"No!" He struggled against the incoming tide, but found himself engulfed in some kind of muck and mire. The stench of it was overwhelming. He became obsessed with the thought of fresh air. If only he could get back to the front—and to the top—maybe he could escape the smell and the sweltering heat.

When Darby had asked her questions about heaven and hell, he'd replied with what he thought was an acceptable answer.

But that was *then*.

All he knew *now* was that when he died, he'd been relegated to an existence outside of time and space. In this unknown location, his situation seemed to be permanent.

"You are here at your own choosing."

Will jerked his head in the direction of the narrow shaft of light that penetrated the darkness, looking for the source of the proclamation. He cupped his hands around his mouth and yelled. "Listen, whoever you are, I'm no fool. There's no way I would have chosen *this*." Surely he would have remembered being given a choice of such magnitude that it had the power to send him *here.*

Met by silence, he called out once more. "Wait! Don't you see? There's been a colossal mistake! I don't understand. A fellow can change his mind, can't he?" He had to get back in control, free himself from the consequences of that crucial past choice by making a *different* choice—a *better* one—this time around.

"Another chance. That's all I need!" He'd get himself out of this hellhole once and for all—Wait! What had he just said? *Hellhole?* No. Not possible. This couldn't really be *hell*, could it? Hell is for the worst of people...for "sinners," right? For killers...child abusers...mass murderers...robbers...kidnappers...rapists...

"I don't think hell is a *real* place," he heard himself say to Darby. "It's just a figment of someone's overactive imagination. There's no such place as *hell.*"

CHAPTER 17

———◆———

TIME—WITHOUT SUN, MOON, OR SKY—WAS endless…meaningless. It just *was*.

Will found himself in a perpetual wait cycle, stagnant among a multitude of bodies, all of whom were unable to move—and only barely able to see. He surveyed his dim surroundings, bodies hemming him in from all directions. They constantly shoved at one another for just a moment's opportunity to bask in the channel of light infiltrating the blackness from above.

He was slowly losing the ability to think, to feel, in human terms. Fighting to keep his sanity, he tried to concentrate on his family—their lives together.

It became increasingly more difficult to visualize the earth— mighty waterfalls, green leaves fresh with dew, sunsets ablaze at the end of the day, a clear brook filled with trout… He lifted his face upward. "Please, don't take my memories away! They're all I have left." He clung to an illusion of wispy clouds floating in the bluest of skies, a baby bird being fed by its mother…

And *sounds*—how he longed to hear the laughter of children, the rhythmic breathing of Brigit sleeping next to him and, of course, music—those strains that feed the very depths of the human soul, that bring joy and peace, that elevate and inspire—that give *hope*.

Most of all he yearned for *touch*. The softness of Darby's skin as he raised her from her bath, the bumpy surface of a golf ball as he placed it on the tee, the smoothness of Brigit's fingers as they caressed his hand in the hospital.

———◆———

The evil here overwhelmed his senses. It multiplied like cancerous cells that could not be stopped. His skin crawled as he experienced it all.

Nothing good, nothing perfect, nothing eliciting smiles or laughter would ever be found in this torturous prison. There was no place here for anything worthy or peaceful. Dignity, strength, and health, did not—could not ever—exist here. He closed his eyes, willing himself to visualize an alternate world for himself where butterflies and hummingbirds danced.

Anger welled up inside him. "Don't leave me here! You've got the wrong guy! Are you listening? I'm suffocating. Doesn't anyone care?"

This doesn't make sense. I never stole anything. I never even had a speeding ticket. I was easy to get along with. I was a good guy, really.

Emotions he had rarely, if ever, experienced in life, began to manifest themselves. Hate…malice…lust… He cringed as the evil desires of others in this space began to invade his mind…desires to kill, hurt, maim, assault, torture…

No matter how hard he tried to escape their presence—resist their power—they would surface and, then, dominate his thoughts. But, more than that, they took on *substance*. He was covered *with* them… permeated *by* them. "Get away! Leave me alone!"

He surveyed his dim surroundings, bodies encompassing him in all directions. He cringed at the pain registered on their faces as they took turns in the light. He cowered, trying to escape from the presence of the guy next to him. Of all the others, his blackness seemed blacker, his smell more offensive. He retched when he realized it wasn't another person at all.

It was *him*.

———————

"Darby," he called. "It's Daddy, honey. Are you there?"

He missed his little girl. She had been such a beautiful baby—fat cheeks, little ringlets of strawberry-blond hair, and her eyes—no one in their family had ever had green eyes.

Darby would start school this fall. Brigit would put her on the bus, but if he knew her, she'd jump in the car and follow it the entire two miles and sit in the parking lot until recess. Then she'd stand next to that giant cottonwood tree just outside the fence, trying to catch a glimpse of their daughter at play. At the end of the morning, she'd drive home and wait for Darby to get off the bus and run to her arms.

"Tell me all about it," she'd say, picking her up and twirling her around...and around...and around.

———————

"Welcome to Hades."

Will shivered at the cackle of someone beside him. "Where?"

"Hades. It's the holding place for—"

"I knew it! No god would send his creation to a place like this— nothing this awful, this hopeless, could last forever." He let out a ragged breath, sighing deeply.

"Soon, we'll have to face Him."

"Who?" Him *who? He can't mean——? Will's* face twitched, a shiver running down his spine.

"God. With a capital 'G'."

Will sighed. Finally, some good news. "Well, that's a relief. I've heard he's all about love…compassion…forgiveness. He'll let us out of here. He'll open the doors and we'll all exit to another world or maybe even get reincarnated. That's what some people believe, isn't it?" Anything would be better than this.

"…it is appointed for men to die once, but after this the judgment…"

The words sent an electrifying charge through Will's entire body. He shook the thoughts away. "Well, that's no problem for *me*, but for some of the rest of you—well, I can see where that wouldn't be such good news. You should have thought more about the consequences of your actions while you were alive."

"You just don't get it, do you?" The guy's raspy voice challenged him.

"Get what?"

He hesitated and then answered Will. "It's probably best you find out for yourself."

"Come on. You brought up this whole judgment thing and now you're not going to let me know how it ends?"

"I just know we're going to be judged for our sins—each one of us. And that, my friend, includes *you.* Hell will be our permanent abode. That's how it *ends.*"

"Well, I'm not a sinner. I'm not like the rest of you."

"Right."

The guy's sarcastic attitude irritated Will. "Darn right."

"If you aren't here because of your sin—because you're waiting for The Great White Throne Judgment and eternal separation from God—then why are you here?" A deep chuckle accompanied his hot, putrid breath.

"It's all a big mistake. Once God shows up, I'll explain everything. I'll be released. Just wait and see."

"Well, good luck with that, Mr. Holier-Than-Thou, but I stand by what I said. You'll see I'm right. Sooner or later."

"For all have sinned and come short of the glory of God."

———————

As a young boy, Will had spent the summers with his grandparents on his mother's side. Besides fishing and playing checkers, he had gone to church with them each Sunday morning. He would sit between them, coloring or completing "dot-to-dots" or mazes while they followed the pastor's sermon in their Bibles.

From the little bit of listening he did, he'd surmised that Jesus was a good guy. But *God?* To be honest, He was hard for Will to understand.

Whereas Jesus was all about love, it seemed like God was more of a disciplinarian. Will was afraid of Him. He wasn't all warm and fuzzy, like his son.

The truth was, the reason he told his parents he didn't want to spend summers with Nana and Papa anymore (somewhere around his ninth birthday) was that he was scared God would come to church one day. He sure didn't want to chance meeting up with Him "face-to-face" like in one of the hymns they sang. No, he could escape that possibility by spending his summers at home, playing with the kids his own neighborhood.

Even back then, he'd been running from God.

—————

Will had received a small Bible at high school commencement. He'd placed it in his father's footlocker after he died. God hadn't healed his dad, so Will had vowed never to go to church, pray, or read that book ever again. Its words might have given his family some measure of comfort during his illness, but at the time he'd thought he was in control—that he could handle things just fine—by himself.

There must have been a warning within its pages, if he'd only looked.

Had *sin* really sent him here? If he was a sinner—and he wasn't ready to concede on that point—then so were others. Why, there couldn't be a person on earth who was *completely innocent*. Of that, he was sure. *So, if some people were sent here, and the others to Heaven, what made the difference?*

"For the wages of sin is death, but the gift of God is eternal life through Jesus Christ, the Lord."

What about Jim and Kelley? Hmm. Well, they were good people, he guessed. He'd seen them and their family going off to church every Sunday morning—all seven of them. But, there had to be more to it than just going to church. Whatever that was, Jim and Kelley had bet their lives on it.

As an adult, Will had believed in living for *now* with no regard for later. He'd given little thought as to his final destination. Sunday mornings were for sleeping in, rather than for heading to church.

Church. In his perception, people went in and people came out. They might have thought they were somehow "improved" but he didn't believe it. Once they changed out of their "Sunday's Best," they were just like him. He saw how they lived. He heard the things they said.

He'd been watching.

———•———

Will needed answers.

A realization bubbled to the surface from the murky depths of his present consciousness. It might be a game changer.

He began to take a good, hard look at his life, going back to the time when he fell into the well at age six. His parents had taken him on a trip across the country to visit relatives. They started out in Kentucky, where Nana and Papa lived, then onward to Ohio to visit his father's family, and finally to Iowa to spend time with Uncle Johnny and his young cousins on their farm.

This was the most fun part of the trip, playing baseball and throwing Frisbees around with the three youngest boys. They all had a great time running around and exploring—doing all kinds of "boy stuff"—while the grownups sipped their lemonade and reminisced on their large back porch.

One afternoon, the boys decided to play Hide-and-Go-Seek in the pasture. After a while, it seemed to Will that he was getting caught more than his share of the time. So, to avoid being "it" *yet again*, he decided to duck under the back fence and hide in a clump of trees he'd seen in the distance.

While cousin Stevie was counting, Will ran for cover. Tripping over an exposed tree root, he fell into an old well. He brought his scraped hand to his cheek, fingers returning with blood. His elbows stung, but the pain was minimal. He panicked, knowing that no one would be likely to look for him there, outside the area where they were allowed to play. It was that lost and alone feeling that had hurt the most—and it had stayed with him throughout the years.

The realization of what he'd done washed over him in waves of fear. He had broken the rule. Now, no one knew where he was.

He screamed for help, over and over, until his throat went dry. He sat down in the wet mud, put his head in his hands, and cried. When he finally looked up, he could see that the sky was beginning to darken. He knew it would soon be night and his chances of being rescued would lessen considerably.

Already cold and hungry, he was overjoyed when he heard first one voice, then others, as they called his name. "I'm down here," he answered.

As his uncle ran back to the house for a rope, his father kept him company by telling him a funny story from his youth. While he knew his dad was just trying to keep his mind off of his situation, he also realized that topside there would be consequences for breaking the rule. Where once he had hoped with all of his might for someone to find him, now all he could think of was how he might be able to escape the inevitable punishment.

Sin? He would have denied it all the way to China and back. But, *now*, it was his constant companion—he was inextricably tied to it. His sin would define who he was forevermore…

———————

Max wasn't here. Will thanked the powers that be that he had been sent to that place resplendent with light, angels, and song. If Hell was real and God was real, then it followed that Heaven was also real. And he was convinced his son was there. His *heavenly* father would take care of him. Will took comfort in that fact. In the midst of his own suffering in this place, he thanked God for saving his boy.

The coming judgment had Will worried, he'd admit that, but if he was ever going to get out of here, he had to get things pushed ahead on God's calendar. He was sure he'd be given some kind of legal counsel to plead his case. When that happened, God would realize that Will had been unjustly charged and let him out—maybe even send him to Heaven where he could be with Max.

He'd need to give his attorney some information that would help with his defense. He'd compile a list of good things he'd done for others—things that would speak to his character—positive things that would *balance out* the wrongs. He needed to dig deep and come up with truly commendable things that would persuade God that he wasn't such a bad guy, after all.

Brigit would testify that he was a good husband. He had a stable job, made a solid living. He hadn't been one to blow money on expensive clothes or cars. He saw to it that the yard always looked good. He'd even gone along with Brigit on her "date night" idea once they'd had kids.

But what would really sway God was humanitarian stuff. Well, there was his involvement in the Special Olympics. Hmm—maybe he could just make up the rest.

Would God know he was lying?

Probably.

He remembered a detective show he'd seen on television once. The guy was advised to plead guilty to the lesser charge in hopes of getting "off" on the one with the hefty sentence.

His spirits soared. That just might work.

He'd plead guilty to being a sinner. He'd already admitted to that much, anyhow—and he'd be cleared of the *greater* charge—being a non-believer.

> **"For God so loved the world that he gave**
> **his only begotten Son, that**
> **whosoever believeth in him should not**
> **perish, but have everlasting life."**

Not *everyone* goes to Heaven. Not everyone makes the *right choice...* Will thought of one of his favorite songs, Sinatra's hit, *I Did It My Way*. He could still hear him croon the lyrics while the big band played.

It's just a song, he told himself. But how many people had been falsely inspired by songs like that—led astray by its clever lines—convinced that *faith in oneself, in the things they did for others, for their community*—was the key to it all?

Had time somehow been suspended in this place? Or maybe accelerated? He thought about Darby. How old was she, now? Was she happy? Did she have a boyfriend? And, Brigit. Had she moved on with her life? Remarried?

Did they know where he was? Was that stupid bumper sticker still on the car?

He loved his family, but he hadn't done right by them. Brigit had tried to warn him. He was comforted by the fact that she'd be saved from all this. And, Darby? Brigit would make sure she knew the truth.

"You will know the truth, and the truth will set you free."

But, what about his co-workers, his neighbors, the bank teller he'd liked so much? A future like his would be inevitable for them, too, unless someone warned them…

He hoped someone would care enough—be persistent enough—like Jim and Derf. No matter how many times they might get the door shut in their faces in the future, he hoped they'd keep knocking… hoped they wouldn't let others delude themselves into thinking they could control their own destiny…play by their *own* rules—deny God.

He had been given many chances to listen. It was his refusal that got him here. He had no one to blame but himself.

He'd often avoided Jim, and even at times told him to get lost. But now he saw the truth in a story Jim once used to illustrate his persistence: "Imagine that our families are going on a camping trip together one weekend. We each have our own wives and children in our trucks, pulling our trailers behind us. We come to a single-lane dirt road. You motion to me to go on ahead with the agreement that you will follow.

"As I turn a corner near the mountain peak, I see that the road ahead is washed out. I manage to pull over, saving my family and myself from our certain deaths in the canyon hundreds of feet below. Knowing you are just minutes from rounding the same curve, I turn around, coming back to warn you of the impending danger. You are able to stop in time. You and your family are saved because you heed my words."

That little story seemed foolish at the time. However, now it made a lot of sense. What one of us wouldn't tell a friend about a dangerous road, a wreck "up ahead" or a non-functioning traffic light? Wouldn't we warn a relative about a child molester lurking in the neighborhood or an unexpected storm?

Yes, the desire to get messages to loved ones was a heartbreaking frustration shared by many now inhabiting this space. Like Will, they were also powerless to warn their family members and friends.

They were tormented by their inability to do so.

CHAPTER 18

———◆———

DRENCHED IN SWEAT, WILL CLOSED his eyes. He envisioned a tall glass filled with ice cubes, the ocean at high tide, a gentle summer rain. He became obsessed with the thought of a cool cup of water. *Please, just—one—drop.* He squirmed in the incessant heat from which there was no relief.

Time stretched out in front of him without end. He thought of prisoners, scratching hash marks on the walls of their cells to mark the days.

The enormity of the chasm between himself and God was more than he could grasp. It would take an eternity to span it—if that was even possible.

The gulf, he realized, was just too wide.

After his father's death, his heart had turned to stone. When Max died, his anger rekindled. He was angry and took his wrath out on God.

At times, scanning radio stations, he had heard the words "God wants to reconcile you to himself." He should have listened. It might have changed things. But, he'd just changed the station to country western and hummed along to a song about a guy doing a gal wrong, instead of hearing about God's unconditional love.

He couldn't deny it any longer. Over the years, God had presented him with many opportunities. Each time, though, he had turned a deaf ear.

He had made his choice. The result was his fault.

Amid the outburst of agitated voices, he shook his fists and shouted toward the beam of light overhead. "God, why didn't you just *force* me to listen? You could have just designed human beings to automatically love you. No choices. You could have been a dictator—a compassionate one, of course. You could have made perfect decisions for all of us."

No blunders, no mistakes, no sin, and no complaints on our part.

———

Will felt lucky to have had a Mom that was a good cook—no, a GREAT cook. Her pastries had won blue ribbons at the county fair every year for as long as he could remember. Her blueberry pie was his favorite and he asked for it each birthday, in lieu of cake. It was that good.

She turned out meals like pot roast, mashed potatoes, fresh green beans, and hot homemade rolls almost every night. Oftentimes, she invited Will's aunt and her family over for dinner.

That's why when his cousin, Marilyn, picked at her food one April night (He knew it had been April because the screen door was open and the crickets were chirping) he just couldn't understand it. What, he wondered, could have made her so miserable?

"Robbie broke up with me." She blurted out all of a sudden, tears splashing into her gravy.

Will's father tried to be sympathetic, making what he thought to be helpful comments between bites of green beans and biscuits. Mom encouraged her to eat. Will didn't have any experience in the matters of love, so he knew better than to open his mouth—it had been full of mashed potatoes, anyway.

Sobbing and, being daddy's little girl, she left her seat and ran to Uncle Jeff, putting her arms around his neck. She ratcheted the whole crying thing up a notch by wailing, "Dad, please make him like me!"

He smoothed her damp hair back from her face and turned to look at his wife. "I sure am glad your mother loves me and you can bet I would have been heartbroken if she had said 'no' after I asked her to marry me. But, honey, if her father had made her say 'yes' when I knew she really didn't want to be with me, I couldn't have been happy living like that. She wouldn't have been, either."

Imprisoned here and waiting for the coming judgment, Will decided, maybe that's how it was with God. He had established this thing called "free will" which let human beings make choices in their lives. Early on, most people learned there would be ramifications for those decisions. There was some guidance along the way from parents, friends—even books—but when it all came down to it, the choices— and the consequences of them—belonged solely to each person.

Like the situation with Marilyn's ex-boyfriend, God didn't command us to love Him. He wanted us to come to Him of our own accord. He let us decide whether or not we were going to trust in Him to guide us, rather than trust in ourselves. He allowed us to accept or reject His message. And, in return, He received love that wasn't coerced or demanded.

His desire was for love that was real and freely given.

Free will...the freedom to choose. Will had always thought it was the American Way. Come to find out, it had been God's way.

The decision he had made not to listen to Derf, Jim, and even Brigit, had been his and his alone. He finally understood. Although he had believed in the *existence* of God, he had denied that salvation had been provided for him—for everyone—through Jesus.

God hadn't sent him here.

It was sin.

The sin of *unbelief.*

When more souls arrived, there was a scuffling—a shifting—to accommodate the ever-growing number. Their cries of pain and disbelief were only too familiar, but Will sensed something different about them. They were defiant—demanding—full of themselves. They caused a major disruption of the status quo.

He knew who they were.

On earth, they were the handsome ones, the clever, the funny, the talented, or the gifted. They basked in their celebrity, enjoying everything earth had to offer. They were worshipped by many, emulated by thousands, envied by all. Their protests echoed those of his own, not so long ago.

They would no longer be at the front of the line, beyond reproach, or rest languidly on their notoriety. They wouldn't be riding in their fancy cars or wearing their flashy rings.

This place was a great equalizer.

"Do not be overawed when others grow rich, when the splendor of their houses increases; for they will take nothing with them when they die, their splendor will not descend with them.

Though while they live they count themselves blessed— and people praise you when you prosper— they will join those who have gone before them, who will never again see the light of life."

Will knew there was a large group of the rich and famous that had helped others. They gave of their time and resources to make life better for those that were less fortunate. Even though some of them had surely gone to Heaven, others had arrived here. He concluded that being sent to Heaven must definitely not have anything to do with "good works" or "human effort."

No. There was more to it than that.

"For it is by grace you have been saved, through faith—and this is not from yourselves, it is the gift of God—not by works, so that no one can boast."

Will noticed a quiet soul hovering next to him. He sensed it was a female. She was in total shock and disbelief, just like he had been when he first arrived. "It's overwhelming, isn't it?"

"I can't be here—in hell! There's been some mistake. Maybe it's a nightmare and I'll wake up in a few minutes in my own bed next to my husband." Her breathless, hurried protests rose to a crescendo.

He pictured her, as she might have been on earth: graying hair in a bun, glasses framing red, puffy eyes. "Try to calm down. If you'd like, I can try to—"

"Calm down? Calm down? Some of you probably deserve to be here, but I don't! And all you can say to me is 'calm down'?"

Will shook his head as he listened to the familiar words. "Of course, you're upset. I was, too, when I first arrived. I still am."

"How long have you been here?" She nudged someone aside to stay close to him.

"I don't know, really. Time doesn't exist here. Welcome to eternity."

"So, this really *is* hell, then? Eternal torment? Separation from all goodness—from God?"

He tried to break the news to her as gently as possible. "Hades, more precisely. It's where unbelievers are held until the judgment."

"You don't understand. I'm not a bad person. I've spent the last twenty years doing everything I thought would insure my salvation."

He felt her distress. "You mean you did things with the hope of earning a place in Heaven?"

"Of course. I did lots of volunteer work at church, at schools and in hospitals. I can't tell you how many meals I've cooked and taken to friends, relatives, neighbors... My husband and I have helped people move, we've babysat their children, participated in walks for different causes, we've—"

"Sounds like it took a lot of time and effort, not to mention money."

"Yes, but it gave us a good feeling to be helping others. We never resented the time or money we spent. And, after all, we knew our 'good works' would pay off. We'd be assured of Heaven—and more."

He shook his head. "I'm sorry things didn't work out according to plan. You did all those things with no reward." *Hmm. Her plan hadn't worked. Somehow, it must all go back to Jesus and what He did...*

"There is a way that appears to be right, but in the end it leads to death."

——◆——

Blood had gushed from Max's gaping head wound. Will's world had turned upside down as he picked his son up and rushed him to the hospital. Once Max was in surgery, he had dropped into a chair in the hematology department and rolled up his sleeve, knowing his son would need life-saving blood.

Many donations were given by people he and Brigit would never meet. Some of them willing to donate blood to help save their son's life had been turned away because their blood wasn't the right type.

Jesus had shed his blood—Will's mother had reminded him of that in the waiting room—to atone for the sins of all mankind. Only the blood of the perfect Son of God could do such a thing. His blood must have been the right type.

He had loved His son, just like Will loved Max. But, God loved us, too, and that compelled Him to send Jesus to the cross. He didn't want anyone to die and go to hell.

Even though he had always doubted there were actually such places as Heaven and Hell, he'd believed in the *existence* of God. But, believing God actually existed wasn't the same as *putting his faith in Him*...placing his eternal life in God's hands.

His boss had trusted him to interview someone and write an accurate story. Brigit had trusted him to be a good husband and father—to take care of their family. Likewise, Christians put their faith in Jesus, God's perfect Son, to save them from their sins.

It was something they could never do for themselves.

All of a sudden, there was a colossal shifting—a spinning—a great upheaval of the balance of things here, beneath. The "earthquake" of sorts, bombarded everyone from all directions. Its great force slammed into them, throwing them around, helplessly.

The belly of the place groaned...twisted...convulsed. Pressure continued to build until it exploded violently, spewing out hot lava. Boulders were regurgitated, releasing torrents of steam.

The resulting screams seemed to never end as blisters and boils covered their bodies. Following a brief period of quiet, the pressure began to increase again, releasing unimaginable energy.

Will crouched down, huddling deep within the masses, attempting to shield himself from hot coals that rained down from somewhere above. If this could happen here, light years away from earth's orbit, Will reasoned that the entire universe had undergone a major event—one too terrifying to even imagine.

The unleashed wrath of the Almighty God.

CHAPTER 19

"Wail, for the day of the Lord is near; it will come like destruction from the Almighty."

MULTITUDES DESCENDED INTO THE ALREADY overcrowded space. Hades pulsated, groaned and enlarged itself once again to accommodate more. Will had never witnessed such an influx at any given time. They all tried to communicate at once. He caught bits and pieces as they pushed past him.

The newcomers chose a prominent orator as their spokesperson. Hushed silence fell over the masses. The man's voice was loud and strong as he proclaimed the news of a most spectacular happening that had started a chain of events of cataclysmic proportions back on earth.

"In the midst of a great storm, the clouds suddenly rifted. We stood, terrified, as their golden edges rolled back. Suddenly, Jesus—in all of His awesome splendor—was revealed. The storm calmed. Not a soul spoke. All eyes were on Him. He descended from the clouds at the sound of thousands of trumpets, playing pure and perfect melodies that created heavenly music beyond description. It was ethereal and delicate, but at the same time, majestic, befitting a king."

Will's heart pounded. What a sight it must have been. *If only he could have witnessed this, then surely, he too, would have believed.*

The orator stopped, momentarily, before continuing his account. "He was clothed in a white robe that appeared to my eyes as 'whiter than white'—so vivid, so pure, that it somehow contained the essence of all colors within it. Golden rays of light burst forth from his hands and feet."

The orator paused, waiting for the murmurs of astonishment to die down. "Accompanying Jesus was a vast multitude of angels, gliding on myriad double-stranded rainbows, shouting His name and praising Him, as if with one voice. The skies were filled with unimaginable light and literally vibrated with expectancy."

What a contrast—the light of truth and goodness—with the darkness here.

He pressed on. "With the eyes of the world upon them, the angels were sent out to all ends of the earth, opening graves, collecting the bodies of believers, and accompanying them as they were lifted into the sky to be with Jesus. As they rose, a kind of energy swirled and pulsated around each one, changing their decayed remains into new bodies of multi-colored light. That being accomplished, Jesus raised his hands once more. He spoke a single word: 'Come'."

The orator broke down then, and wept at great length. "I cried because I knew He was not calling *me*. But, at the sound of this invitation, Christians from every corner of the world were raised into the heavens, being transformed as they rose, into radiant beings. Their bodies were resplendent...iridescent... Their faces glowed and from their lips flowed the most beautiful songs. As they reached Him, their individual voices came together, collectively, creating one magnificent outpouring of praise. We sensed it would never end." Exhausted and overcome by his account, the orator collapsed.

Another soul nearby came forward to continue the narration. After clearing his throat, he spoke boldly. "This miraculous event, this spectacle of power and love, ended just as suddenly as it had begun. People of every nationality heard the King's final words in their own language. He said, 'I will come, again.' Then Jesus and His believers evaporated into thin air and the clouds were rolled back into place."

He gave time for the magnificence of the event to sink in before continuing. His voice quivered, beginning softly, and building in intensity until it resonated throughout all of Hades. "We stood there, gazing toward Heaven, crying and weeping. Then people began to run through the streets, screaming. Some threw themselves off cliffs and into the sea. In the end, a numbing coldness settled over the land. Sin and evil began to rule there as never before. The last shred of goodness and decency had vanished from the earth and we understood that the end was near."

The new arrivals started shouting all at once. Each one blurting out his own perceptions of the chaos that followed.

"Quiet! One at a time." Will's own voice stilled the masses.

As order was restored, the crowd calmed down. Each was given an opportunity to add details about what life had been like from then on.

They gave reports of rivers gone dry, entire countries without adequate amounts of drinking water. The sea had overflowed its boundaries, ocean life cascading onto land and dying in heaps all over beaches—spilling over into nearby neighborhoods.

The newcomers described giant insects prowling the land and attacking humans with their deadly venom. They said the pain of those bites never subsided.

Reports came of wildfires burning unrestrained, consuming homes, vegetation and human life for thousands of miles. Earthquakes were commonplace. Volcanoes erupted sporadically; hot lava running through the streets of villages and into fields, destroying treasured grain.

Stars fell from the sky, crashing onto the earth and wiping out whole cities. Huge gaping holes in the earth coughed up sulfurous gas, killing in an instant. Weather patterns also changed. Seasons no longer existed. Hurricanes and tornados ravaged neighborhoods and cities all over the world. Frequent power outages left many freezing to death because of the sub-zero temperatures in winter. Even deserts were frozen over at times.

In sharp contrast, gasses from warheads used in conflicts among the nations caused such intense heat as to melt human eyes. They literally ran down their victims' hollow cheeks. Their throats burned so badly they couldn't speak.

Will cringed as the news of widespread destruction continued. *Had Brigit and Darby escaped this devastation? Had they been spared this horrific pain?*

Half of the world's population had been annihilated. Vast numbers of people lay uncared for in the streets. When they died, their bodies were stacked on the sides of the roads. There were too many to bury—and not enough able-bodied workers to ever accomplish the task.

There was a scarcity of food and clean water. People were starving to death and forced to eat human flesh in order to survive.

It seemed there was a military leader that promised world peace—and for years people followed him. He was an eloquent speaker and very persuasive. People around the world were duped by his message. Because of him, world leaders had been ousted and whole governments overturned.

He was Satan's puppet. He began his reign by brainwashing people into believing that he had all of the answers, and he was capable of ruling justly—with compassion and wisdom.

He ordered that microchips be placed into the back of each person's hand containing all of their personal information: name, birth-date, social security number, income tax, political party, church affiliation, bank account numbers, and so on. All of this was needed, he told them, to establish an international database, which would be accessed only in the case of emergencies. In addition to allowing fluid travel around the globe, it would be used to find missing persons, identify bodies, and flush out terrorists.

This seemingly harmless—but incredibly convenient database—was praised by government leaders and citizens alike. It was embraced by nearly everyone as a convenience—not recognized as the tool of ultimate control and destruction that it eventually came to be.

Many were duped into thinking that taking the chip—the Mark of The Beast, as it came to be known—onto their hands or foreheads was a good thing. Others, who refused its implantation, were kept from buying any kind of goods, including food. Their bank accounts were frozen. Insurance was cancelled. They lost their jobs and were denied an education. They became prisoners in their own homes until they were forced to live on the streets due to falsified non-payment of their mortgages.

People barricaded themselves inside their homes to escape the rioters and rebels that created havoc in the streets. Crime and looting was prevalent. It was every man for himself.

Will put his hands over his ears. He couldn't bear hearing any more. But, then, he had to know...

Disease ravished human life around the globe. Entire families were afflicted with the pain of flesh-eating bacteria and other untreatable diseases. They begged for death that would not come. Others fled to the sanctuary of caves and underground tunnels while Satan and his vast demonic army devoured everyone in their path.

Max had been spared the horrible things happening on earth. Will envisioned him safely in Heaven where peace blanketed every soul. He hadn't witnessed the destruction of the world.

No, his son's eyes were filled with the wonder of lush green vegetation, exotic flowers, and rainbows that could be climbed. He might even be able to walk through those mesmerizing bands of vivid color. He'd visit unimaginable waterfalls, rest on wispy clouds, and see everything in super-vivid dimensions.

He'd be privileged to walk with Jesus, experiencing, firsthand, what it's like to be loved completely and unconditionally. He was in the company of other believers—his grandparents, Jim—one of the best neighbors he'd ever known—and Derf, his faithful friend.

Surely Max's sister and mother would be there by now, too. He reassured himself that they were among the throng caught up to meet Jesus in the air. What an experience it must have been for them—all because Brigit was persistent and determined to learn the Truth.

And that Truth had set them free.

———————————

Electrifying energy, akin to a bolt of lightning, lit up all of Hades. It ricocheted around the perimeter and cast eerie shadows of black, putrid green and sickening yellow. Semi-solid clumps burned, sizzled, and then dropped from above, giving off sulfurous gas. Columns of steam swirled together forming heinous images that took on lives of their own.

Will covered his mouth and eyes with his arms as best he could, holding his breath at first, then finally giving in to fits of raspy coughing. The light waned and slowly died. He paused, appreciative of the darkness and the way it masked the ugly truth of his abominable existence.

As much as possible, he still tried to live in the past—at least his memories of it—which was all he had left. It was the simple, everyday things that he missed the most: snuggling under the quilt on a winter's morning, sunlight filtering through the bedroom window, the feel of moist earth between his fingers.

Like the faces of his grandparents, those vivid recollections had slowly begun to dissolve. Perhaps his memories would soon fail to provide an escape from the reality of this place.

———◆———

Will had heard about an area where a strong band of "quasi-believers" congregated. His inquisitive journalist nature prompted him to press through a sea of bodies in hopes of finding someone who might know about the motivation for Jesus' return trip.

He interrupted their hurried conversations as he approached. "Would any of you be willing to answer a few questions for me?"

"What do you want to know?" A loud voice bellowed nearby.

"I heard the news about how Jesus came to earth and took believers back to heaven with Him. I was told He intends to return to earth, again. My question is simple: 'Why'?"

"The question may be simple, but the answer is more complex."

"Oh?" Will sighed. He had been hoping he'd get a quick answer and then be on his way. He wasn't sure he was up for another long oratory.

"I'm Garrett. I wrote eight best-selling books on the subject of prophecy and the so-called 'end times.' Two were even made into movies. These were not *Christian* books, you understand. My platform was one of skepticism of everything Christian doctrine stated about God *after* the creation of the world."

"So, you felt God created everything and pretty much left us on our own after that?" *I wasn't the only one...*

"That's it, in a nutshell. I spent a lot of time studying the Bible, finding what I thought were flaws, and then debating that very fact, and other Christian claims, with a great many Bible scholars over more than a decade."

"Some people don't even acknowledge that God exists," Will interjected.

"True. But, most people hear about God from their parents, friends, or in church. Others—people in remote parts of the world—are said to be aware of His existence through creation itself. Scripture says even the rocks and the trees will cry out to testify of Him if we human beings fail to!" Garrett's voice boomed, loud enough for all assembled nearby to hear.

"And His creation of the world?"

"It's all in the very first book of the Bible, Genesis 1:1 'In the beginning, God created the heavens and the earth.' The rest of the book is a chronicle of the order in which He created everything, including mankind. It tells how God provided for their every need. But, man was disobedient and sin came into God's perfect world. It formed a chasm between the perfect Holy God and his creation."

"My wife, Brigit, said that God's desire was for a relationship with man while he lived on earth."

"Right. He also had a plan for having man join Him in Heaven. But that could only be possible if there was way for man to be absolved of his sin."

"Well, wait a second," Will interrupted. "In between crossword puzzles and doodling, I listened to the preacher's words when I was a kid. He said back in Bible times God accepted sacrifices from people in order to cover their sins. Am I wrong?"

Garrett wiped drops of sweat from his brow, licking his parched lips to moisten them before he continued. "No, but that's *all* it did—*cover* the sin. It never really got *rid* of it. When people sinned again, they'd have to sacrifice—again. Man was caught in a never-ending sin/sacrifice cycle."

"So, that's where Jesus came in?" Will sucked in a deep breath. He had pushed this very message aside time and time, again. Now, in this desolate place, his heart began to race, his soul at last hungry to hear the message of salvation.

"He became the final, complete, and perfect sacrifice for mankind's sin—for all time and eternity. After his crucifixion, God raised him from the dead on the third day. This fulfilled God's plan to redeem each and every human being by the shedding of *Christ's* blood. You see, only the Son of God had perfect blood—untainted by sin—that would satisfy God's requirement for the *remission* of man's sins."

"So, you're saying God provided His *own sacrifice?* He gave up Jesus for *us?*" Will gulped. *For me...*

"That's right. Romans 5:8 says '...God showed his love for us, in that **while we were still sinners**, Christ died for us.' So many people miss that simple truth—you and I included. "

Will scratched his head. "So, salvation was His *gift* to us—no strings attached?"

"All we would have needed to do was ask for forgiveness and confess Jesus as Lord—meaning acknowledge that He paid our ransom, so to speak." Garrett hung his head.

"So, this selfless act by God's Son made man 'right' with God?" Will's shoulders heaved as the words pierced his heart.

"Romans 10:9 says 'If you confess with your mouth the Lord Jesus and believe in your heart that God has raised Him from the dead, you will be saved—"

From an eternity in Hell.

CHAPTER 20

WILL FOUGHT AGAINST THE FORCE of the swelling throng to stay by Garrett's side. "Hey, you never told me why Jesus plans to return to earth."

"Ah, you're right. This is a future event—one of the very ones I'd been debating against for years. Now that I'm *here*—and even though it's too late to make a difference for *me*—I can finally acknowledge the truths I previously rejected. I'm going to answer your question from my new viewpoint—that of a believer.

"Anyway, now that all of the Christians are in Heaven with Jesus, there's a series of things that will take place before Christ goes back to earth. By the time He does, though, some more folks back home will have become believers. There will be a huge battle—the mother-of-all-battles—in which Jesus and his angels defeat Satan and his demons, who are subsequently thrown into the Lake of Fire.

"Simply put, He goes back to rid the world of evil, once and for all. The victory is His. He creates a new Heaven, and a new earth, where he sets up His kingdom, reigning for all eternity."

Looking back on his life, Will decided he would have done things differently, if he had known what the future held—Max's death...his own cancer diagnosis...

"In a way, we *were* able to know the future," a soul nearby said.

Had he stated his conclusion out loud? He turned away from Garrett, distracted by the voice behind him. "What do you mean, exactly?"

"I mean the information was available. We just didn't care enough to pursue it. Or, we thought we knew it all, or wanted to live life our own way—putting off making a decision about Jesus until 'tomorrow.'"

The guy was piquing Will's curiosity. Okay, he'd bite. "So, where would we have gone to obtain such information?"

"The one and only source would have been the Bible."

Why hadn't he seen that coming? He really didn't need any more reminders as to how badly he'd screwed up. "No offense, but how'd you end up here, if you knew all you claim?"

"You don't recognize my voice?" he asked.

A Southern drawl... "Should I?" The guy's voice sounded vaguely familiar, but he just couldn't place him.

"You worked in the cubicle across from me for several years. We had some good times, you and I."

"Randy?"

"The one and only."

"A religious editor, *here?*" *How can that be?*

"Who would have thought, huh?"

"You should be the last person I'd meet up with." He'd always liked Randy. He had been a fun guy, always joking and having a good time. It didn't make sense. *Was Randy really here among all these unbelievers?* "What happened?"

Randy grabbed onto Will's arm to avoid being tugged into the quagmire of drifting souls. "All those jokes I used to tell about Christians showed how I *really* felt. To me, they were duped, brainwashed hypocrites. But, I did my job. I laid out the religious pages, wrote the copy, and took the pictures. I even went to some of their church services. I sat in the front row, sang the songs, and followed along in the Bible. I even put a dollar or two in the plate on occasion."

"What was the problem?" Will wanted to know—had to know—it was research for his future defense.

"I didn't believe a word of what I wrote. Every time they talked about sin and how it separated us from God, I thought they were talking about the 'other guy.' Surely, it didn't apply to me. I knew I was far from perfect, but a downright sinner—no way!"

There it was, straight from Randy's own lips. His very words—the ones that Will had envisioned using in his opening arguments—rang true. Will was no different from Randy. Neither one of them had allowed the seed of truth to take root in their hearts.

Just like Randy, he had no defense.

———◆———

Within moments, the entire cavern convulsed. Hot lava spewed from its bowels, running in scalding rivers throughout the abyss. Again and again, Will cringed at the ear-splitting explosions. He screamed, along with the others, as the molten spray seared into their flesh.

The subterranean space shook with such force that it created a vivid picture in his head of the earth being knocked off its axis. Wave after wave of souls flooded in. Whatever was happening on earth was killing thousands of people each second. Could this horrific catastrophe be the battle between Jesus and Satan—between good and evil—between the power of God and the power of the grave?

———◆———

Will's breathing became labored, dredging up memories of the panic attacks that plagued his childhood. They usually happened when confronted with an oral exam or when he had to give a speech. He'd feel light-headed, have difficulty catching his breath, and his heart would beat erratically anytime he was thrust in front of the class-room. His world would spin, beads of sweat forming on his forehead and upper lip.

"Take a drink of water and a few deep breaths," his well-intentioned teacher would say. Other times she'd send him to the nurse's office to calm down.

But, there was no nurse's office for him to retreat to in order to diminish the effects of the panic attack that was building now. It was much more severe than any he'd had in the past. He closed his eyes and took in a series of calming breaths. He ended up choking, however, as hot bile burned his eyes, nostrils, tongue and lips.

He writhed, struggling unsuccessfully to break through Hades' ever-growing numbers and run away—one final time. Just as he had feared talking in front of the class, he now dreaded facing the eternal God.

"Whoever believes in him is not condemned, but whoever does not believe stands condemned already because they have not believed in the name of God's one and only Son."

He was guilty.

He'd been given his share of second chances. No one could bail him out of this. He had nothing to look forward to but an eternity of pain.

He finally acknowledged the truth. Brokenness and remorse would do him no good. He was overcome with shame and guilt. Just as he had longed for physical death to bring him peace and rest from his suffering on earth, now he cried out for the end of his very existence. Oh, that God would simply reduce him to miniscule particles of dust and blow him away with His mighty breath.

———•———

The day of accounting had come. God's book of records would be opened. All here would be judged. And, they would pay the penalty. The time for grace and mercy were long past.

Will held his breath as the names were called and, like prisoners, they were marched out of the pit. His eyes riveted on the tall golden doors as they opened. One by one, each person who entered was absorbed by the pure light emanating from the throne room. Their cries began almost immediately—even before the great doors shut behind them.

Outside, the crowd shrank back against the walls, lest they be the next one called to the Judgment Seat. Their collective whimpering roared throughout the chamber.

Will waited with the rest of them to hear news of each verdict. His heart pounded in his chest as he listened for an acquittal, but each time the doors swung wide, the prisoner was ushered to his swift and sure punishment. Heads hanging, resigned to their fate, their eyes looked different somehow, as if they understood—*and even agreed*—with the accurateness of their sentencing.

Each person's life was being individually evaluated and each one's punishment, in varying degrees, was consistent with that evaluation. They would be separated for all eternity in Hell—from God and all that comes with His goodness.

Will accessed what was left of his pleasant memories: making pancakes with Brigit on Saturday mornings, breathing in the scent of spring flowers as he and Darby lay napping in the hammock, he and his father sneaking the last of the cold pizza for breakfast, enjoying a snack of ginger snaps and ice-cold milk with his mother while sharing the events of his day at school.

A shiver ran down his spine as two footmen halted beside him. The taller of the two thrust out his claws, his yellow eyes boring into Will's as he situated him between the two of them. Each time he faltered, they snatched him up, set him back onto his feet, and pushed him forward.

One of the footmen produced a multi-corded whip. He had already used it countless times, when other prisoners had tried to flee the hour of their judgment. He licked his lips and glared at Will.

Knowing better than to resist, Will straightened his shoulders and lifted his chin. He was determined not to show his overwhelming fear to the others as he walked past them.

When the Golden doors were opened, however, he fell to his knees. He raised his hands to shield his eyes against the brightness of the glory surrounding the Great White Throne.

As the edges of the clouds overhead rolled back, he viewed a tender family scene from times past. A young mother sat on a straw floor, among the sheep and cows, cradling her little one. She stroked the child's soft dark hair and brushed his cheek with her fingertips.

Her husband stood to the side, talking in hushed tones to several men wearing robes of fine linen and head coverings encrusted with brilliant jewels. The array of gifts they placed nearby contrasted sharply with the meager surroundings.

The young mother placed the sleeping boy gently on a bed of sweet hay. As she stood watching Him, the others joined her, bowing their knees in reverence, as they worshipped The Christ Child.

The scene changed. The child, now grown, was nailed to a cross by Roman soldiers and lifted high above a crowd of weeping people. The gray-haired mother, eyes filled with sorrow, fell at the foot of the cross as she witnessed her son's crucifixion.

As the final scene unfolded, a large stone rolled away from the mouth of a cave and out walked the risen Jesus—triumphant over sin and death—the King of Kings and Lord of Lords.

Now, in the presence of the Living God, Will cowered. Cloaked in sin, guilty and without excuse, his eyes met the Savior's—full of anguish and sadness.

He hung his head as the great Book of Life was opened.

**"If you declare with your mouth, 'Jesus is Lord,'
and believe in your** heart that God raised him from
the dead, you will be saved. For it is with your heart
that you believe and are justified, and it is with your
mouth that you profess your faith and are saved."

Romans 10: 9, 10

Dear Reader,

Thank you for reading, *The Choice*. I trust that it will serve a vital role in preparing your heart for all the goodness God has for you!

This book was important for me to write because I could no longer stand aside and allow false teachings and misconceptions to influence life-altering decisions about God's judgment of sin and the reality of Hell.

Like Will, we are also faced with The Choice: to one day stand before God, forgiven by Jesus, and therefore enter eternity in Heaven, or be found guilty and face an eternity in hell.

I encourage you to make your decision based on the standard by which God will judge all men: faith in Jesus Christ.

Just as Heaven is a real place, Hell also exists.

My prayer is that you will accept God's gift of salvation. (If you are already a Christian, perhaps sharing this book with family and friends will provide the basis for discussion.)

Please continue your journey by reading The Bible, starting with the book of John. Find a good Bible-preaching church to attend and someone you trust to mentor you as you begin your new relationship with Christ.

My website is on the back cover. I'd like to hear from you.

Written with you in mind and in the blessed assurance of God's Word,

Brenda Poulos

Verses quoted in *The Choice: Will's Last Testament* are from The Holy Bible.

"Enter through the narrow gate. For the gate is wide and the road is broad that leads to destruction, and many enter through it." Matthew 7:13 NIV

"It is appointed to man once to die. After this, the judgment." Hebrews 9:27 NKJV

"For all have sinned and come short of the glory of God." Romans 3:23 NKJV

"The wages of sin is death, but the gift of God is eternal life through Jesus Christ, the Lord." Romans 6:23 KJV

"For God so loved the world that he gave his only begotten Son, that whosoever believeth in him should not perish, but have everlasting life." John 3:16 KJV

"You will know the truth, and the truth will set you free." John 8:32 NIV

"Do not be overawed when others grow rich, when the splendor of their houses increases; for they will take nothing with them when they die; their splendor will not descend with them. Though while they live they count themselves blessed—and people praise you when you prosper—they will join those who have gone before them, who will never again see the light of life." Psalm 49:16-19 NIV

"For it is by grace you have been saved, through faith—and this is not from yourselves, it is the gift of God—not by works, so that no one can boast." Ephesians 2:8,9 NIV

"…God showed his love for us, in that while we were still sinners, Christ died for us." Romans 5:8

"There is a way that appears to be right, but in the end it leads to death." Proverbs 16:25 NIV

"Wail, for the day of the Lord is near; it will come like destruction from the Almighty." Isaiah 13:6

"Whoever believes in him is not condemned, but whoever does not believe stands condemned already because they have not believed in the name of God's one and only Son." John 3:18 NIV

"If you declare with your mouth, "Jesus is Lord," and believe in your heart that God raised him from the dead, you will be saved. For it is with your heart that you believe and are justified, and it is with your mouth that you profess your faith and are saved." Romans 10: 9,10 NIV

ABOUT THE AUTHOR

—◆—

A FORMER TEACHER AND ELEMENTARY school guidance counselor in Arizona, Brenda Poulos's first book, *Runaways: The Long Journey Home,* was published in December, 2015. Based on a recurring dream, the story of Jake and his dog, Hound, has the power of forgiveness as its central theme.

Brenda is a member of American Christian Fiction Writers and is current president of Christian Writers of the West. She and her husband have four adult children, seven amazing grandchildren, a lovable rescue cat and a sixteen-year-old dog that divides his time between napping and chasing the cat.

Brenda volunteers at an elementary school, hospice, and her church. She enjoys reading, movies, interior decorating and home renovations. One project follows another as she and her husband constantly look for yet another home in need of a little TLC.

As a Christian author, Brenda's goal is to communicate God's love to her reading audience. You are invited to connect with her on Goodreads.com, and at www.spiritualsnippets.com, where she focuses on "Seeing Life's Events in the Light of God's Word." She offers new writers encouragement on www.brendapoulos.org and www.5scribesandtheirstories.com, a website she shares with other members of her critique group.

Manufactured by Amazon.ca
Bolton, ON

12721455R00129